M000073048

I LOVE YOU,
I HATE YOU,
DROP DEAD!

Books by Artie Shaw

THE TROUBLE WITH CINDERELLA

I Love You,

I Hate You,

Drop Dead*!*

*V*ARIATIONS ON A THEME BY

Artie Shaw

BARRICADE BOOKS INC. / NEW YORK

Published by Barricade Books Inc.
150 Fifth Avenue
New York, NY 10011

Copyright © 1965, 1997 by Artie Shaw
Preface Copyright © 1997 by Artie Shaw
All rights reserved.

No part of this book may be reproduced, stored in a retrieval system, or transmitted in any form, by any means, including mechanical, electronic, photocopying, recording, or otherwise, without the prior permission of the publisher, except by a reviewer who wishes to quote brief passages in connection with a review written for inclusion in a magazine, newspaper, or broadcast.

Printed in the United States of America.

Library of Congress Cataloging-in-Publication Data

Shaw, Artie, 1910–
    I love you, I hate you, drop dead! : variations on a theme / by Artie Shaw.
           p.   cm.
    ISBN 1-56980-101-0
    I. Title
PS3569.H37412   1997
813' .54—dc21   96-48095
                                     CIP

First Printing

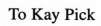

To Kay Pick

Contents

Shortly after I began playing a horn, I found myself making up rules for myself. Things like "When you get to be the best musician in a band, quit and join some other band." I followed that rule for about six years, until I ran out of bands. (Most of the bands around in those days weren't much good anyway.) Eventually, though, I got good enough to become one of the two or three top lead alto saxophone and clarinet men in the New York radio studios, which in those days was the highest-paid work you could get as a musician.

The problem was, most of the stuff we had to play (aside from an occasional recording session) was so atrocious that I finally couldn't stand it any longer. By that time, I was twenty-two years old and so disgusted with the music business that I started taking extension courses in literature and creative writing at Columbia University, hoping to learn enough to become a writer or perhaps a teacher. (Or *something*—anything to keep from having to go back to that goddamned radio garbage.) After a year or so of concentrated study, I figured I had learned enough to try to write a book. (God knows what I expected would happen if I ever did get it written.)

Anyway, I bought a dilapidated little farmhouse on some scrubby acreage out in Bucks County, Pennsylvania, and moved out there to see what I could do. It took me a year to find out I needed to know a hell of a lot more than I did, so I went back to New York and eventually—I'm doing a good bit of skipping here—decided to form a band of my own to see if I could do a little better with that.

Within a few months, I learned a lot, but most of it had less to do with music or writing than it did with what I was going to have to do to find an audience who would put up with my views on the kind of music I felt a good band should play. Some years later, I finally did write a book— about that as well as a number of other things—called *The Trouble with Cinderella*. This book you're holding in your hands is my second, and it's just been republished after some thirty years.

By the time this one first came out, though, I had formulated a number of new rules dealing with various subjects. One was called "Five Simple Steps to Become a Genius." (What the hell, I figured, might as well aim at the top while you're at it.) Here are the steps:

1. Find yourself a genius.

2. Make friends with him.

3. Follow him around.

4. Watch what he does.

5. Do it.

That fifth rule is, of course, the toughest one, and to make it even tougher, there's no guarantee you'll ever be a genius. One thing you can bet on, though: if you keep at it long enough, you'll get pretty good at whatever it is you're trying to do. And you'll certainly know quite a lot about what it takes. Remember, I said five *simple* steps, not easy ones.

Actually it's still a perfectly valid formula. All the geniuses I've ever known or heard of—from William Blake to Matisse to Louis Armstrong—had to spend a great deal of time and effort to get as good as they were at what they did. In fact, I'm convinced that the ability to keep working at something for as long as it takes is one thing all geniuses have in common. Talent is another matter, and that can help, but talent is simply the ability to do with relative ease what other people find extremely difficult. Besides, talent alone does not necessarily make you a genius. Genius is like perfect pitch; either you're born with it or you haven't got it. (In fact, I believe there are people with perfect pitch who never even realize they have it.) The important thing to bear in mind about geniuses is that they all keep right on working at what they do despite the ridicule, scorn, and even hostility (or worse, total indifference) of most people they encounter. And it can take as long as a couple of centuries before some works of genius are recognized. Even an acknowledged genius like Michelangelo remarked (when he was eighty-two): *"Ancora imparo"*—meaning "I'm still learning."

I tried my damnedest to follow those five little rules; and ultimately I learned an important lesson. When it comes to music (or literature or any other art), you're not in a footrace. All you can do is become the best you can be at what you do. That alone will take you the rest of your life.

And so . . . there came a time when I met Sinclair Lewis. This was shortly after he'd become America's first literary Nobel laureate. Like many people of that era, I had read everything he had written and admired him. So I made friends with him and began following him around and watching what he did. Pretty soon I discovered there was one thing he did every day. He went into a room by himself, closed the door, and began writing; then he threw out most of what he had written, rewrote what was left, and kept doing that until he got it to say what he wanted it to. So I started doing that, too, and guess what. A couple of years later, I ended up with a book of my own. It wasn't too hot when I finished it, but I kept rewriting stuff and throwing out most of what I'd written, and finally it got good enough to be published.

Boy, look at this, I thought when I got my hands on the first copy. A real live book!

After that I started this one. And then another. And another. And here I am after all these years, still at it. As the Bible says: "Of making many books there is no end."

And so, now that most of the people in this one are gone, I guess it's OK for me to reveal who they are—or were. The point is, I disguised them, acting on a tip from my friend Sinclair Lewis who, when I told him that many of the people I knew well enough to write about were quite well known, said, "That's no problem. If you're writing about a tall thin man, make him a short chubby woman."

Well, I didn't go *that* far, but I did disguise them pretty well. Enough so that no one (except some of the people who actually played a part in one or another of these stories) recognized who they were.

The first story, "Grounds for Divorce," is mostly fiction. The incident on which it is based did happen, though, and was reported in the newspaper *PM* about the time America got caught up in World War II. It was just a blurb, about a man who'd been held up and made a deal with the holdup man to buy back an item of sentimental value by offering to pay him a far larger sum for it than it was worth. The holdup man agreed. But when they met the following day, the man told him he'd been unable to raise the money that quickly and asked if he could have one more day. The holdup man said OK, and the rest of this story was more or less what actually happened.

For some reason the story bothered me. I couldn't stop thinking about it and wondering what had gone on *behind* all that. Finally I decided to make up a story to explain it, basing the principal characters on people I knew. The victim was a music publisher whose name wouldn't mean much to anyone today, so there's no point in mentioning it. The description of the holdup man is that of a farmer who used to be a neighbor of mine when I ran a dairy farm up in Dutchess County, New York. He was one of the most formidable-looking men I've ever known. Over six foot six with scarcely an ounce of fat on him and one of the gentlest men I've ever met.

Then, when I felt that the story would require a *reason* for what happened, someone to talk the holdup victim into doing what he finally did, I used a stunning *Vogue* model I knew (again, I won't mention the name because it's irrelevant, and besides she's still alive). After that I made up a commentator based on a writer friend named Frederic Morton, who'll probably be astonished to learn he's the "Fred Wilkinson" of this story. Incidentally, I've since rewritten this one, at much greater length, omitting the commentator and letting the holdup man tell *his* story, and renamed it "The Best of Intentions"—which is also the title of my third book. I'm not sure now which version I like better; and to complicate matters even further, another, truncated version of it appeared in the April 1964 issue of *McCall's,* almost a year before this book was published.

In story number two, "Old Friend," I used myself as the narrator, called him Billy Miles, and made him a pop singer—which is about as far removed as I could get from myself, since I've never had the faintest desire to be what we used to call a "boy singer." As for the principal male character, I made him a WASP and located him in Chicago in order to misdirect readers into thinking he might be someone like Nelson Algren or James Farrell or even Carl Sandburg, rather than William Saroyan, which is who he really was. The woman he married was Carol Marcus, and she is now married to the film actor, Walter Matthau—who has absolutely nothing to do with any of this. However, the story is as close as I could get to what Carol herself told me, as well as to what happened a bit later, when my old friend Bill Saroyan came to New York and pleaded with me to try to persuade Carol to remarry him. (I was the one who had introduced him to her some years earlier, and despite everything that took place as a result, Carol and I have remained the best of friends.)

As for the ending of the story, that is precisely what happened when I showed Bill an early draft of it, without the present ending. Bill read it very rapidly, then turned to me and said what he says at the end of this story, which struck me as precisely the right ending, so I used his words, almost verbatim.

The third story is called "Whodunit" because I couldn't, and still can't, tell you who did what to whom. Two of the people are (or were) quite well known. The man is based on John Houston, and the woman was based on Kathleen Winsor, whom I would have gladly pushed off that cliff myself after the shabby trick she and her bloody lawyer, Arnold Krakauer (whom she then married, and who, shortly thereafter, I was happy to hear, died), contrived to extort a rather large sum of money from me when we got divorced, even though she had already made a bundle from her first book, *Forever Amber.*

Here, the narrator is based on a man I once knew in Hollywood, named Lester Koening, who is also dead. He was an "assistant" (or "associate producer"—or however his screen credit read) to Willie Wyler who produced and directed a number of hit films, including *Ben-Hur, The Best Years of Our Lives,* etc.

So there you have some of the dark secrets behind these tales. One last point: my original title for this book was *Boys and Girls Together,* which seemed to me a quietly sardonic comment on three novellas about people who are anything but "together." But then about the time the book was being readied for publication, something awkward occurred. A novel by William Saroyan appeared, called *Boys and Girls Together,* and I had to come up with a new title. I decided to call my book *I Love You, I Hate You, Drop Dead!* which I think is a fair enough summation of what these stories are all about.

Artie Shaw

September 16, 1996

I LOVE YOU,
I HATE YOU,
DROP DEAD!

Grounds for Divorce

We were about halfway through lunch when Buddy Ross suddenly went "*Psst.*"

I looked up.

"Don't look now, Fred," he said, examining his plate intently, "but you know who just walked in?"

"What . . . who?"

"*Sshh,*" he said. "Just keep on eating, will you? Tell you in a second."

"What goes on?" I asked after a moment.

"Marjorie," he said out of the corner of his mouth. "She just came in. I'd just as soon she didn't see me."

"Oh?" I said. I had heard about Marjorie but had never met her. I went on eating.

He stiffened. "Too late," he said. "She spotted me. Here she comes."

I heard the sound of her high heels as she approached.

"Why, Buddy," I heard her say. "How *are* you?"

I stared at her. I had had no idea she was so pretty. I suppose I must have looked a bit surprised. But she was not looking at me. She stood there beside our table with a little smile on her face.

Buddy was on his feet. "Fine, Marjorie," he said. "I'm just fine. How are *you?* You look wonderful."

"Why, thank you," she said. "I *feel* very well."

They stood that way for a moment, looking at each other. I was standing up by now and beginning to feel awkward.

"Oh, yes," Buddy said, half turning to me. "Fred, this is my—" He checked himself embarrassedly and then said, "I mean—this is Marjorie. . . ." He paused, looked confused, then said, "I'm awfully sorry, Marjorie. I guess I just can't think of your husband's name."

She laughed. "Bennett," she said.

"Of course," Buddy said, laughing a little. Somehow, neither of them seemed to be laughing at anything funny.

"It's a simple enough name," Buddy was now saying. "I don't know how I could have—"

"That's perfectly all right," she said.

I stood there.

"Well . . ." Buddy said. "Anyway . . ." turning to me— "Fred, this is Mrs. Bennett. Fred Wilkinson, Marjorie."

"How do you do," I said.

"Won't you join us for a minute, Marjorie?" Buddy asked.

"Why . . ." She glanced uncertainly around. "I'm meeting Helen Washburn for lunch—you remember Helen Washburn, don't you, Buddy?" She looked at me, smiled, and said, "Please sit down, won't you?" Then, looking back at Buddy— "Both of you, please sit down."

All three of us remained standing.

"Oh, all right," she said. "I suppose I can see her from here when she arrives."

Buddy drew out a chair for her. She sat down, waited for us to be seated, and looked brightly from one to the other of us. "Now then," she said. "I hope I'm not interrupting anything?"

"Of course not," Buddy said.

"Not at all," I said politely.

She gave me a smile and turned to him. As she did, something peculiar happened to the smile. It was still there but now it changed subtly, I could not quite tell how. It seemed to freeze and become not so much a smile as a kind of mask. Buddy must have noticed it too because he began to make conversation as if to bridge an awkward gap.

They both gabbed on for a while, almost compulsively, as if the one thing on earth to be avoided at all costs was silence. They went from Helen Washburn on to someone else, I can't remember who, but after a while they seemed to run out of words at about the same moment.

At that point there was a brief silence. I looked up. She was staring down at the tablecloth, nervously crumbling a bit of bread in her hands. Her red-lacquered fingernails moved busily as she kneaded the bread into a small wad. I glanced at her face. She was unquestionably a very pretty girl but at the moment there was the suggestion of a frown on her face. I looked at Buddy, saw him looking at me, and turned my eyes back down to my plate.

Presently she said, "Oh—there's Helen." She sounded relieved. "She's looking for me." She waved toward the entrance. I looked over and saw a tall, well-groomed woman standing there. Just then the woman spotted us, smiled, and waved back.

Marjorie stood up. Buddy and I got up too. For a moment they stared gravely at each other. "Well, Buddy," she said, "It's nice to see you looking so . . . so well."

"Thanks, Marjorie," he said, taking her hand and smiling. "You look pretty sharp yourself, honey," looking her up and down.

It seemed to embarrass her. Women do not flush easily these days, at least not in my experience, but she seemed to flush as his eyes went appraisingly up and down her smartly-dressed figure. I had to agree with him. She certainly did look sharp. She wore a simply-cut black dress and a string of small pearls that looked quite genuine to me. There were a number of other little appurtenances all of which had two things in common—they seemed to belong right where they were and they looked very expensive. Mr. Bennett evidently did right well for himself, whoever he was.

Buddy kept right on looking her over. After a few seconds the flush on her cheeks, or whatever it was, faded. She gave him one last look as if she wanted to say something, then gently took her hand away from his.

"Thank you, Buddy, I'm glad you think so." She turned to me. "Nice to have met you, Mr. ah—"

"Wilkinson," Buddy prompted her, "Fred Wilkinson."

"Thanks," I said. "Nice to have met you too," and she left the table, her high heels clicking as she walked away.

"Whew," said Buddy.

We both sat down again.

"That was *weird*," he added, looking reflectively off in the direction she had taken.

"How do you mean, weird?" I asked.

He did not answer. There was a thin film of sweat on his forehead. He stared right through me, his big eyes looking even bigger through the thick tortoise-shell glasses he wore. He had the look of a man peering at something way off in the distance.

I repeated my question.

"What?" he said. "Weird? What do you mean, Fred?"

"You said something was weird."

"Oh?" He stared blankly at me for a moment. "Did I?" All at once he came back from wherever he had been. He laughed. "It's all right, Fred. You don't have to look at me like that."

"What the hell goes on?" I asked.

"Nothing . . ." He shrugged. "It's the first time I've run into her since we were divorced is all." He grinned wryly. "Feels kind of funny, you know?"

"I suppose it must." There was a short silence. "She's a very good-looking girl," I added.

He nodded absently. "Yeah, she is, isn't she?"

"How long's it been?" I asked.

"How long's it been?" he repeated vacantly.

"The divorce," I said.

"Oh . . ." he said. "About three years ago. We were separated in . . . let me see now. September, 1959, it was."

I sipped my coffee. When I looked back up at him he was staring curiously at me.

"You've been married about ten years now, haven't you, Fred?"

"Twelve next May," I said. "Why?"

"I don't know . . ." He looked over my head and said, "It's *funny*. You know, for a while there I was positive Marjorie and I were going to make it."

"Oh well," I said lamely. "I guess it's one of those things everyone thinks. For some people it works out. Others—well, how's anybody going to know, when you come right down to it."

He gave me an odd look. "I think *I* know," pausing and then, "now anyway."

I laughed. "What's the secret formula, Buddy? Let me in on it, will you?"

"No, but seriously," he said. "I think I really do know. At least I know one thing for sure."

"What's that?"

"I know exactly why Marjorie and I couldn't make it. I don't know whether I could explain it but I do know exactly how and why and when we came to the end of it. Hell, I can remember every last detail of it, like total recall."

"I don't know," I said. "Maybe so, but I don't think anyone ever knows just what it is that breaks up a marriage. I'd have a pretty tough time believing it was ever any one thing. An accumulation of a lot of little things would be more like it."

"No, Fred," he insisted. "I believe that's really all it ever is, just one thing. Only trouble is, most people won't let themselves see it when it happens."

"Maybe that's the whole formula," I laughed.

"What is?"

"Not to see it. Not to let yourself see it. Or—if you have to see it—why, just making yourself forget it."

"Nice work if you can do it," he said. "But sometimes you . . . Oh, hell, I suppose it's the usual story. It depends . . ."

"Yes, that's about it, I guess. It depends. . . ."

We sat quietly for a while. I happened to look across the restaurant at one time and there was Marjorie at a table over in a corner. She was sitting with the other woman and both of them were laughing. She suddenly looked over and caught me staring at her. She stopped laughing and made one of those meaningless little social gestures people make when they are too far away to speak. I saw the other woman glance over at our table and turn sharply away. I nodded, smiled foolishly at Marjorie, and turned to Buddy.

He was staring down into his coffee cup. As I looked at him he raised his eyes and said, "Listen, Fred. I'd like to tell you something."

"Why, of course, Buddy. What's up?"

He hesitated for a moment. "I've never told anybody else about this . . ."

"What's it about, Buddy?" I asked. "You and . . . ?" I nodded toward that corner of the restaurant.

He bobbed his head and said, "Yes—in a way it is. In another way, maybe it isn't. I'd kind of like to see what you think. Do you mind?"

"No, I don't mind."

"You in any hurry, Fred?"

I looked at my watch. "I've got a couple of hours. That long enough?"

"Sure—plenty," he said.

"O.K., shoot."

He called the waiter, ordered another pot of coffee, and began.

"I guess from what I've said you're probably expecting one of those intimate confessions or something."

I shrugged.

"Don't worry," he laughed, "it's nothing like that, Fred. It's a pretty weird yarn but I think when you've heard it you'll see why Marjorie and I broke up. Anyway, it's the only way I can explain it. You'll either see it or you won't. In any case . . ."

The waiter came back with the coffee. Buddy asked me if I wanted some, and when I shook my head he poured himself a cup, added sugar, and took a sip. While I waited for him to continue, I thought back over the fifteen or sixteen years since I first met him.

At that time I was about thirty. Buddy had just come to New York City and gone to work as a staff writer on one of those radio and TV fan magazines that used to be around by the dozens in those days. Just in case "staff writer" sounds impressive, I should add that in Buddy's case it was a title and very little else. Even so it is not too easy to explain how he got the job. (I believe I remember having heard that his father knew someone connected with the publishers, or something of that sort.) He was fresh out of Dartmouth and looked it—right down to the crew haircut and everything that went with that.

But like many small men, Buddy had lots of drive. At first meeting you might not be apt to spot it. What you saw was a naïve, bumbling, very earnest little fellow, with that standard Brooks Brothers look about him. He had all kinds of energy. He was always tearing around on those stubby legs of his shooting off sparks in all directions and generally behaving as if he were right in the center of some enormously significant, world-shaking project—though the chances were that he was only on his way to interview some third-rate actor appearing on some second-rate television show.

Still, there always was a rather likeable quality about Buddy. "Cute" is the word I have heard girls use about him; and on the whole it is an accurate enough description. I remember how I used to smile to myself at the wide-eyed way he went at New York City. In fact, long after I came to realize that beneath that wide-eyed manner he was a very shrewd little operator with at least one of those wide eyes of his right on the ball at all times—even then, I used to enjoy running into him at odd moments here and there around town.

But all this was quite a while back. Buddy has come along since then. He is now executive editor of *The Continental Review* (circulation 6,000,000) and, from all I can gather, he has managed to maneuver himself into a pretty strong position with his publishers. I have recently heard rumors that he is next in line for the top spot on the magazine and I know of no good reason to doubt the rumors.

No question about it, Buddy has wised up a whole lot during the past fifteen years. There are lots of other ways in which he has changed. The wide-eyed manner has long since been dropped by the wayside and along with it most of the naïveté. Curiously enough, though, in many respects he remains essentially the same bumbling little fellow he was when we first met; which may account for the fact that over the period I have known him he has managed to get himself into and out of some of the most peculiar scrapes you would be likely to hear of outside the pages of a James Bond novel. I can only suppose he must derive something from all these little off-beat adventures. Perhaps he even enjoys them. There is no other way I can understand how any man can get himself embroiled in so many odd situations. Yet whenever anyone mentions the subject to him he only grins and makes some joke about "gathering material for a book." By this time the whole matter has become a more or less stock gag, which he himself seems to relish more than any one else.

A good many of these "situations" have revolved around women—that is aside from the three years he was married. For some reason I have never been able to understand, Buddy always attracted neurotic women as though he were a qualified psychoanalyst. Perhaps they feel some obscure impulse to mother him—or something. Whatever it is, it has certainly never appeared to bother him a bit. Time and again I have seen him come up fresh and unperturbed after one or another of these unholy alliances with some of those Weird Sisters he is constantly getting himself involved with. And each time, he emerges from the entire slightly mad business with the same air of unruffled guilelessness that got him into the idiotic snarl to begin with.

There are a number of things about Buddy Ross I have never quite understood. In lots of ways, come to think about it, he is something of a weirdie himself. But this particular episode he told me about was pretty far off the beam, even for him. It has clung like a burr in my mind ever since. I cannot seem to shake it off, yet at the same time I do not know exactly what there is about it that troubles me. All of which may be no more than an indication of my own confused values. For whatever else my feelings about this whole affair are, they are certainly quite complicated, and I would be the first to admit that my own sympathies may well be entirely misplaced. The point is, though, I am not even sure I understand what those sympathies are, exactly—let alone what they mean. . . .

"This thing started when Marjorie and I'd been married almost three years," Buddy resumed. "I was on my way home from a poker session I used to sit in on with five or six other guys once every couple of weeks or so. It must have been about three A.M. when the game broke up. I grabbed a cab and got out at the corner of Park and 89th and started walking east. We lived about halfway between Park and Lexington and I was just walking along, not thinking about anything special except maybe how I'd got pretty well cleaned out in the game that night. There was nobody in sight, that hour—the street looked deserted, you know? Then all at once I heard these quick footsteps coming up behind me. I turned and saw this big heavyset fellow in a topcoat and a dark brown hat pulled down low over his eyes. He was only a few yards away. I stopped for a second and all of a sudden I saw that he was pointing a revolver at me."

Before he could quite take in what was happening Buddy heard a low voice saying, "All right, Mac, hold it right there."

Without thinking Buddy took a faltering step back.

"Hold it, I said," came the voice again. Buddy held it. The man's voice was quite steady and calm, almost matter-of-fact, but there was something altogether businesslike about the way he stood off a couple of paces holding the point of the revolver unwaveringly on Buddy's chest.

"Say, what's the big idea?" Buddy asked.

"Take it easy, Mac, you'll be O.K.," the big man answered quietly. Buddy thought he caught the barest shadow of a grin on his face. It was too dark to be sure but somehow it made him angry. Of course there was nothing he could do about it. He stood there fighting down his rebellion at being forced to submit helplessly—"like some kind of a flat-footed jerk," as he put it.

"Now then, if you'll just step into my office over here," the man was indicating a narrow alleyway between two apartment houses, where he had apparently been hiding, "we'll get this over with and you can be on your way."

Buddy hesitated momentarily.

"Come on, Mac—let's go," the man's voice prodded.

There was nothing to do but obey. As he went ahead into the alleyway, hearing the man's heavy footsteps a pace or two behind him in the dark, Buddy's anger unaccountably disappeared and he became aware of a curious thing.

"Naturally," he told me, looking into my eyes with that bad-little-boy expression of his, "I couldn't see the guy behind me and there was no way of knowing what he might be up to, whether he was going to slug me or not, but for some crazy reason I wasn't even scared."

Instead, he went on to say, he began to feel a strange, almost pleasurable, sense of excitement. All at once he found himself beginning to enjoy the situation in some curious way.

When they had gone several yards into the alleyway he heard the man say, "O.K., Mac, this'll do it." Buddy turned to face him. In the darkness he could make him out only as a dim bulk looming up a few feet away.

"All right, mister," Buddy said, "would you mind telling me what this is all about?" Not that he did not already know, of course.

"Nothing too serious," the other repeated. He had an astonishingly gentle voice. "Only," he went on, in what Buddy described as a "fatherly tone"—"I wouldn't try any monkey business if I were you, Mac. This little gadget's loaded, understand? No sense in any accidents happening, is there?"

Coming under those circumstances, the words had an absurdly melodramatic sound and though he was fully aware that there was nothing very funny about any of this, Buddy had to grin to himself.

"It was the word 'accidents' that did it, I guess," he explained. "Sounded like something out of Mickey Spillane or something and all of a sudden the whole damn thing struck me as terribly funny, you know?" At that moment, he added, he seemed to regain complete control of himself.

"Look here," he said quietly, "I don't want any trouble, fella, any more than you do. Suppose you tell me what you're after and I'll try and oblige. Fair enough?"

"Fair enough," the big fellow agreed, his heavy voice calm and low. Well, at least, Buddy thought to himself, he's not one of these hopped-up characters that might start shooting because he's scared out of his wits.

"Sounds like we're going to get along just fine," the big man was saying. "Nice of you to be reasonable about it."

Without a doubt, Buddy now said to himself, this is the suavest stick-up I ever did hear of.

The big fellow had just said something else.

"I beg your pardon?" Buddy asked politely.

"I said how much you got on you?"

"Oh . . . not much, I'm afraid."

"*How* much, Mac?"

"About eight dollars is all."

"Let's have it."

Buddy dug into his pocket and produced the money.

"What else?" the man asked affably.

"Nothing much," Buddy said. "A wallet, only there's nothing in that but a few papers and cards, stuff like that. You know, driver's license, that kind of junk. Let me see now. . . . Oh, yes, some keys and stuff. But I guess you wouldn't be interested in those, would you?" he added helpfully. "You see, I'm just on my way home from a poker game and I happened to hold a few bad hands so . . ."

"Yeah. Can't win 'em all, can you?" the big man nodded agreeably.

They stood in silence for a moment. By now Buddy's eyes had become accustomed to the darkness and he could see the man a little better. He was at least four inches over six feet tall, and heavy-set. "But," Buddy added, "he didn't look like a guy to tangle with. Nothing flabby-looking about him."

The man's face was shadowed by the pulled-down brim of his hat but from the little Buddy could make out it seemed to be an average enough face, neither handsome nor ugly. His whole bearing was perfectly assured, easy, even pleasant, like that of a person engaged in an ordinary business transaction.

"Say, Mac, what's the time?" he asked casually.

Without thinking, Buddy drew out the thick, old-fashioned watch he always carried and held it close to his eyes. Before he quite knew what was happening, the big fellow reached out and took it.

"Thanks, Mac," he said, slipping the watch into the pocket of his topcoat.

"*Hey! Wait* a second, what's the big idea?" Buddy burst out.

The man waggled his gun once.

"Look here, now," Buddy went on in a lower tone, "you can't have that. That watch is mine, it was a—"

"Easy, Mac. Easy does it," the other cut in. His voice was still calm but it was no longer gentle. Once again the gun waggled menacingly. Buddy and he confronted each other tensely. Suddenly the man took a swift backward pace and nodded toward the mouth of the alleyway.

Buddy stood his ground. "Listen, fella," he said stubbornly, "I told you I don't want any trouble. But that watch happens to be—"

"The watch is mine, Mac," the man said flatly. He nodded toward the sidewalk again. "Come on."

Buddy started to say something but the man cut him off with an impatient waggle of the gun. "Wha'd'ya say we break this up, Mac. Come on, let's get moving."

Buddy took a long, deep breath and stood where he was. "Look, fella, hold it just one second, will you?" he pleaded.

The man paused. "Yeah?"

"I'd like to make you a proposition."

"Proposition? What kinda proposition?"

"About that watch. . . ." Buddy began.

"Not interested," the man cut in, once more waggling his gun. "Come on, let's go," he said, jerking his head brusquely toward the sidewalk.

Buddy knew he was beginning to stretch it rather thin but still he made no move.

The man looked at him steadily.

"I'm warning you, Mac. Don't start anything." His voice was as low as ever but now there was a bite in it.

At this point in his story Buddy stopped abruptly and stared off over my head. He made me think of a chubby little owl as he gazed off into space through those heavy shell-rimmed glasses. After a moment he went on.

"You know, Fred, that was a pretty peculiar couple of

seconds. What the hell, I've never thought of myself as an especially brave character. All I knew was I just wasn't going to let him get away with that watch, that's all. Of course I could have easily got my head knocked off right then and there, I suppose, but as it turned out. . . ."

As it turned out he obviously had not, despite his obstinate refusal to budge. His next words, he now told me, seemed to come from some area inside himself of which he had never had the slightest awareness. Something seemed to be driving him on, some strange force which he had no time to examine closely at that moment and which, later on, when he tried to re-examine the whole business out of sheer curiosity, had vanished completely, leaving behind no more than a queer, shaky feeling in the pit of his stomach.

"Look here, mister," he told the man, "I'm not trying to start anything. I told you I'm not looking for trouble. But if you don't listen to what I'm trying to tell you, there's going to *be* trouble—plenty of it. I mean it."

The gun stopped waggling now. It held very still, its snout aiming directly at Buddy's chest. He felt his whole body tighten with the tension, his belly muscles stiffening as he waited.

The big man stood immobile, his shadowed eyes boring into Buddy's.

"Listen, Mac," he said slowly, his voice suddenly flat and hard, "you're liable to get hurt bad."

"All right, fella," Buddy answered in a calm voice he scarcely recognized as his own. "That's up to you. I guess I'll have to take my chances." He stopped and waited, watching the other intently, every nerve in his body taut.

Nothing happened. Not one single thing. For the first time, the big man's assurance seemed to flicker. It was only for the shadow of an instant but it was enough for Buddy.

"Now you might as well listen to me," he went on, "because I'm dead serious. Either that or you might as well start using that gun right now. I'm not kidding you one bit, fella."

And the odd part of it, he assured me with a twisted little grin, was that he meant every word.

For a moment after that there was a thick silence during which he felt his heart pumping crazily and the blood roaring in his ears. Suddenly the big man let out his breath in a heavy sigh. He began to shake his head from side to side, slowly, as if he were both puzzled and relieved at the same time.

"You're a funny guy, Mac," he said, and after another moment, "O.K., let's hear it. But make it snappy—fellow doesn't get too much leisure time in this racket, see?"

Buddy started talking fast. "All right. Look, I'm not squawking about the few dollars I gave you. Keep it, I don't care about that. But that watch is something I—*wait* a second, let me *fin*ish, will you? That watch is important to me. My father gave it to me just before he died and it means a hell of a lot to me. I want to make a deal with you."

The man was eyeing him dubiously. "What kinda deal you got in mind?"

"Here's the proposition," Buddy hurried on. "Take a look at the watch yourself. It's not worth very much, you can see for yourself. I don't believe you'd be able to get more than twenty or thirty dollars for it anywhere. Plus a chance of getting caught trying to get rid of it."

"Go ahead, I'm listening."

"All right. I'll make you an offer. I'll give you fifty dollars for it. How's that?"

The man stood quietly, his expression noncommittal.

"All right—make it a hundred," Buddy said. "Fair enough?"

Still no answer.

"Well? How does that sound to you?" Buddy asked.

A brief pause, then, "Let me get this real straight, Mac," the man said slowly, an odd new quality in his voice. "You say the watch is worth a hundred to you?"

"That's right."

The man nodded. "And you say you're willing to give me the hundred for it? Right?"

"You heard me," Buddy answered impatiently.

"Yeah, sure I heard you," the man rasped. "Real clear I heard you. . . ," his voice suddenly taking on a harsh, tight sound. "Now you listen to me, you cheap little chiseling bastard, and hear me real good for a change. When you handed over that dough I took your word. I didn't even frisk you. Then I trick you into pulling out your watch and you start beefing your goddam head off. O.K., I still don't frisk you. You say you're a guy doesn't want any trouble, I take your word for it and I'm about to let you go on your way without no trouble, like I told you in the beginning. So now you're going to pull something fancy. Gonna be real cute, that it? I told you not to pull nothing, didn't I? Didn't I warn you, no monkey business? *Didn't* I, you no-good little son of a bitch?"

"*Hey*, what are you driving at? I don't get it!" Buddy put in, dismayed at the sound of pure hatred that had crept into the man's voice.

"Come on, you little chiseler, cut out the bullshit! Get it up!" the man snapped. The gun began to rise. "Come on, move, before I—"

For the first time, Buddy felt a wave of real terror surge over him. He stood rooted, speechless.

"Listen, Mac, if you think I'm kidding around—" The gun was now pointing steadily at a spot somewhere in the region of Buddy's eyes. "Where's that hundred bucks? Come on— get it up, before I start working on you." He started to come forward.

"*Listen!*" Buddy said frantically. "Listen to me, for God's sake! You've got me all wrong, fella. Listen, I haven't got any hundred dollars *on* me. That isn't what I meant."

The big fellow eyed him. "What the hell are you yapping about?" he growled.

"All I meant," Buddy said swiftly, his words tumbling over themselves in his hurry to get them out, "—all I'm trying to say is, I'll *pay* you a hundred dollars for it. I'll meet you wherever you say. You say where and when and I'll be there and give you a hundred dollars for it. That's all I meant. I won't mention it to anyone, I'll do it any way you say. All I want is the watch, now do you understand?"

As he spoke he saw the man's expression change. When he finished, the other slowly shook his head from side to side several times.

"Who you trying to kid, Mac?" he said at last.

"I'm not kidding, believe me," Buddy said. "That watch means a lot to me. Look, I realize all this is nothing to you one way or the other. But why not give me a break and let me work out something with you? What can you lose?"

This time the big man laughed out loud. He gave Buddy an incredulous look. "You know, Mac—damn if I don't believe you really mean it."

"Of *course* I mean it," Buddy told him.

The man said nothing.

Buddy asked, "Well, what do you think?"

The man regarded him gravely for a short while. Finally he said, "I'm trying to figure the angles . . ." his voice trailing off as he looked quizzically at Buddy.

"What's there to figure about?" Buddy urged. "I told you—you can't get that much for the watch anywhere. This way you'll be getting a hundred dollars for it. How can you—"

"Look, Mac—how do I know you won't try to cross me?"

For a moment Buddy could not think of anything to say. Oddly enough, up to now the thought had not even entered his mind.

"Oh," he said, "I see what you mean . . ." He let it hang there lamely, unable to think of any way to reassure the fellow.

The big man watched him stolidly. Buddy's thoughts darted in little concentric circles. In the end he could find no way of breaking the deadlock.

"What about you?" he asked at length. "You got any idea how we might work it?"

The man shook his head absently.

"Would you be willing to make the deal with me if you knew I wouldn't double-cross you?" Buddy persisted.

"I'm trying to think about it, Mac," the man said slowly. "Let me figure a minute."

Buddy waited.

Presently, "Tell you what I'll do, Mac. You sound like an honest guy." Buddy felt an impulse to smile but fought it down. "O.K.," the man said after a short pause. "Maybe we can work out something."

"Fine," said Buddy gratefully. "Any way you want to do it."

Another moment of hesitation, then, "All right—here's what you do, Mac. Get the hundred bucks and be at Ryan's Bar and Grill tomorrow night between eight-thirty and quarter of nine, got that? I'll find you."

"Ryan's Bar and Grill," Buddy repeated. "Tomorrow night between eight-thirty and quarter to nine. All right, where is it?"

"Third Avenue between Fifty-Fourth and Fifty-Fifth. West side of the street. You can't miss it, there's a big sign in front."

"Good enough, I'll be there."

"O.K.," the man said briskly. "And look, Mac," his eyes boring directly into Buddy's, "I'll be watching you real close, understand?"

"I told you," Buddy said earnestly, "all I want is my watch and you can take my word I won't do any—"

"Yeah, I heard you," the man interrupted. "All I'm saying, don't try anything cute or you can kiss the watch goodbye, understand?"

"Don't worry," Buddy said, "I'll be there with the money."

Suddenly the man began shaking his head slowly from side to side and laughing softly, deep in his throat.

"What's up?" Buddy asked.

"If this ain't a hell of a note," he grinned down at Buddy. "Maybe I'm soft in the head but hell, long as we're making a deal I might as well go all the way with you." He took a short step away, lowered the gun, and slid it into his coat pocket. "There you are," he grinned. "See? I'm taking your word, Mac."

"Fine," said Buddy grinning back up at him. "I want you to know I appreciate your confidence." Both of them laughed at this.

The man stepped aside now, motioning to Buddy to precede him out onto the sidewalk. As they emerged from the alleyway Buddy felt a sudden impulse.

"Shake," he said, sticking his hand out.

The man hesitated, gave Buddy a quick searching glance, grinned sheepishly.

"O.K., Mac, it's a deal," he said, clasping Buddy's hand in a firm grip.

He turned and strode rapidly toward the end of the block. Buddy watched him until he disappeared around the corner of Lexington Avenue, then started home.

Marjorie was asleep when he let himself in. He thought of waking her and telling her what had happened but decided it could keep till morning. He undressed quietly, got into bed, and eventually fell asleep.

Next morning, at breakfast, Buddy told Marjorie the whole story. When he finished she sat there staring at him with a sort of astonished look on her face.

"Honestly, Buddy," she said at last, "if you aren't the limit."

It was the last reaction he had expected. "What's the matter now?" he asked. "Can I help it if some guy comes along with a gun and decides to—"

"No, not that," she said. "That isn't the point. Though I must say, if there's something peculiar going to happen within a radius of fifty miles I can count on you to get yourself mixed up in it somehow."

He grinned at her. "Well, at least it makes life interesting."

She made a face. "Interesting," she mocked. "I hope you aren't counting on ever seeing your watch again."

"Certainly I'll see it again," he said indignantly. "What are you talking about? I told you, I'm going to meet him tonight and get it back."

She looked at him and let out a little tinkling laugh. It annoyed Buddy. He had not had much sleep and his eyelids felt scratchy. But the main reason for his irritation was a sudden suspicion that she might be right.

"O.K.," he grumbled as she went on laughing. "Let me in on the joke. What's so funny?"

She stopped laughing and stared at him again.

"Buddy, you don't really think you're ever going to see that man again, do you?"

"Why not?" he demanded.

"Oh, honestly, Buddy. Do you think he's an absolute idiot?"

"Well, if he isn't, I suppose that makes me one, is that what you're driving at?" His voice rose.

"Buddy! Calm yourself. What's wrong with you this morning anyway?" She began laughing again.

He watched her peevishly for a moment, then gulped down the remainder of his coffee and stood up. "O.K., Marje, I can see there's no sense discussing it with you." He started huffily toward the bedroom. As he finished dressing he became aware of Marjorie standing in the doorway. She was smiling at him.

"What's funny now?" he said.

"You, my love. You're funny."

"Yeah, I know. Must be a riot living with a comedian. Nothing but laughs all day long."

She came in, sat down on the edge of the bed, and watched him fussing sourly with his bow tie.

"Don't be an old grouch," she said presently. "I think you behaved very bravely, darling."

"Gee whiz, thanks a heap," he said. "Buddy Ross, boy hero, that's me." He finished tying the bow tie and went to the closet for his jacket.

"Oh, Buddy, I was only teasing." She went into a sort of baby talk. "What is it, did I hurt its feelin's? Is it feelin' all angry and misunderstood?" Ordinarily she was able to amuse him with this, but today it only irritated him further.

"Come on, Marje, cut it out," he said.

She continued for a while longer. By now Buddy was actually beginning to work up to a small rage. He turned on her and as she saw the look on his face she stopped smiling.

"Why, Buddy," she said, her eyes wide. "You're really angry, aren't you?"

"Listen," he said hotly. "I'll make you a bet. I'll bet you anything you want to name that I'll get my watch back."

"So that's what's bothering you," she said. All at once she threw her head back and began to laugh. He stood there glaring at her.

"Oh, my," she gasped, going off into another spasm of laughter. "You really do expect that man to meet you. I can't—oh, you're so funny." She was unable to go on. She fell back on the bed and dissolved in a burst of helpless laughter.

"You know something?" he said, looking furiously down at her as she lay there gasping for breath.

Finally she managed to say, "What, darling?"

He looked at her. Her face was pink with laughter, her eyes were wet, and she looked terribly pretty sitting there on the edge of his bed. Buddy thought to himself, three years, it's almost three years we've been married.

"What is it, Buddy, why are you staring at me like that?" She was still not quite over her laughter.

He started toward the door. In the doorway he paused, turned to give her one last look, and saw her still smiling at him.

"You *stink*," he said, eyeing her coldly. He turned abruptly and stalked out of the apartment.

Several times that morning he thought of calling home and telling her he was sorry, but each time he thought of it he censored the impulse. He nursed his anger, hugged it to him, till by the time he went out to lunch he had succeeded in convincing himself he was completely justified. He had also managed to convince himself that he had no doubt whatever about the man's showing up that evening with the watch. Immediately after lunch he went to the bank, drew a check for one hundred dollars, cashed it, and went back to work.

It was six o'clock when he got home. Marjorie was in the living room, reading a magazine. She looked up as he came in.

"Hello, grouchy," she said.

He nodded briefly, mumbled a hello, and went into the bedroom. He began to take off his clothes in preparation for a shower before dinner. As he hung his suit in the closet she came in.

He glanced over and saw her examining him curiously. He said nothing.

"Did everything go all right today, dear?" she said.

"Yeah," he grunted.

He could feel her looking at him but he went on with what he was doing, paying no attention to her as he removed his shoes and socks.

"Buddy," she said.

"What?"

"Are you still angry?"

"Me? Hell no, what's there to be angry about?"

She came over and stood next to him. He got up, started past her toward the bathroom, but suddenly she reached out and took his arm.

"Buddy," she said again.

This time he looked at her. They both looked at each other for a moment. Suddenly he began to feel a little ridiculous. They both started laughing at the same time. In another minute they were over the whole thing.

During dinner Marjorie said nothing further about that morning's conversation. The meal went off peacefully. After dinner they walked into the living room and sat down. Buddy lit a cigarette. Marjorie watched him for a moment as he settled down in his chair. She started to say something, opened her mouth, then closed it again.

"All right, Marje," he said after a few seconds. "Come on—what's on your mind?"

She hesitated. "You won't get mad?"

He laughed. "No, honey. I told you, I'm sorry about this morning. What were you going to say?"

"I've been thinking, Buddy," she said slowly. "About this morning. About your being so sure that man will be there with your watch. And I was thinking . . . well, maybe you were right. Maybe he will be there. . . ."

"Yes?"

She looked at him.

"Well, I was wondering. Suppose he does come? Have you decided what you're going to do?"

He reached into his pocket and took out the hundred dollars. The bills were stacked neatly. They were tens, crisp new bills, and he held them up so she could see.

"You mean you're actually going to give him the money?" she asked.

"Naturally," he said. "Why not? I told him I would."

"But Buddy! He's a criminal. You don't make promises to a criminal and then keep them. It's not the same as . . . ."

"Not the same as what?"

"I don't know. It just seems—funny. After all, he stole your watch. It isn't as if you had made some business arrangement with him. I don't see why you feel you owe him anything."

"I don't feel I owe him anything," Buddy said. "Hell, far as that goes he doesn't owe me anything either. I made a deal with the guy, in good faith, now it's up to me to go through with my end of it. After all, it was my idea. I was the one who talked him into it. He could have told me to go to hell. He's the one that's sticking his neck out to do me a favor, when you come right down to it."

"But he stole your watch, darling. It's your watch, not his."

"Look, Marje, you don't understand. I made a deal with the man. I gave him my word. All right, I know it's outside the law, actually, but that isn't the point. This is a simple matter of two people agreeing to do certain things. It's a kind of—call it a pact, sort of. I wanted my watch back, he agreed to take a hundred dollars for it."

She gave him a peculiar look and shook her her head.

"Well, come on, you may as well say what's on your mind, Marje," he said irritably.

"Do you really want me to?" she asked.

"Of course—I'm asking you to."

"Very well. It may not fit into your code of—oh, ethics, I suppose is what I mean. But if it were up to me I'd see to it that the man was put away where he couldn't go around holding people up at the point of a gun. He's a criminal and according to my code of ethics criminals belong in jail. . . . You asked me, remember."

"Yes, I asked you. And that's all you see in this whole thing? A criminal who should be in jail?"

"What more is there to see?"

Buddy thought a moment.

"There's lots more. I see it as an agreement I entered into. Sure, I know the guy's a criminal, but the criminal part of it was all over last night. When he had that gun on me and took the watch out of my hand—sure, at that time he was a criminal. Right then, if there'd been any way to do it, I'd have had him put away."

"That's all I've been saying, Buddy."

"Yes, I understand what you've been saying. But that isn't all there is to it. Don't you see? All right, sure he stuck me up. But he was taking his chances there. He was stacking himself up against the law, against society, any way you want to put it. If he were caught he'd wind up in jail. O.K. But as it happened, he won—don't you see that? And once he'd won, I had only two choices. One was to let him get away with my watch. The other was to do what I did and hope he'd be decent about it. Yes—you don't have to look at me like that. I mean it. Decent."

"Oh, Buddy, honestly," she said.

"What's wrong with it?" he demanded. "Seems to me it makes sense. Maybe not ordinary sense but still, does that mean it's got to become all distorted and out of focus. Seems to me a promise is a promise. What would you have me do now, turn around and be a—a—well, a Judas or something? I wouldn't have any respect for myself if I were to turn him in after I've already given him my promise not to. Hell, if I were to turn him in now—I don't know, seems to me I'd be nothing but a louse. Sure, he's a criminal. But I'd a hell of a sight rather be a criminal than a louse. At least a criminal has a certain dignity."

"Don't get so excited, Buddy," she said smiling at him. "You don't have to get so excited about it."

He stood up and began pacing up and down the room.

"Of course," she said, after a few moments, "I see what you mean about the promise you made. It's only . . ."

"You just don't understand why I should feel obligated to keep a promise to a criminal," he interrupted.

"Something like that," she said. "But we needn't go into it now. I can see you're too excited to talk about it calmly."

"Listen, Marje," he said hotly. "Just listen to me, will you?"

"Why, of course, darling. Of course I'll listen." She looked up at him.

"Will you just take my word for it that I know what I'm doing."

"Why, of course I will," she said. "If that's all you want."

He controlled himself. "It's not all I want. What I'd really like is . . ." but he could not find any way to say what he really wanted. He felt baffled, unable to communicate with her, and as a result he began to get angry again.

"Buddy, please," she said. "I just said I'd take your word."

"But you still don't see it, do you?"

She smiled. "No, to be perfectly honest with you, I don't. It seems to me simply a matter of throwing away a hundred dollars on some silly whim. But of course if it means that much to you . . ." She shrugged.

He looked at her and fought down a strong desire to go over and slap her hard across the face.

"Yes," he said instead, "it means that much to me."

There was a rigid little silence.

"That is," he added, unable to restrain his sarcasm, "unless you have some pertinent suggestion."

She raised her head and looked right into his eyes. "As a matter of fact," she said, "I do."

"Please," he said, with a little bow. "By all means, let's hear it."

She hesitated. "Well," she said at last, "if you're really interested . . ."

"Please," he said again, sitting down across the room from her. "I'm interested."

Ignoring his manner, she began speaking quite seriously. "Very well, Buddy. This is what *I* would do, if it were up to me. Since this whole question of good faith seems to mean so much to you—please, Buddy, let me say what I have to say . . ."

He subsided and she went on. "It seems to me the first thing is to find out just how much good faith this—this man is ready to show *you*. Until you know that, you can't know anything."

"Well?"

"Why don't you go over there and see if he does come, and then—if he does—why not tell him you couldn't raise the whole hundred dollars today? And that you'll get the rest tomorrow and give it to him then, if he's still willing to go through with his end of the arrangement."

"What are you trying to get at?" he asked.

"I'm trying to give you another day to think about it, if you must know," she said. "Perhaps by tomorrow you won't be so—well, emotional about all this. Also, you'll at least know once and for all whether you're merely being quixotic and foolish about something quite simple which for some unknown reason you're insisting on building up into a complicated matter of ethics, good faith, and Lord knows what-all else."

"In the first place," Buddy said, "I didn't bring ethics into it—that was your idea. In the second place, suppose it is a matter of ethics? Why deny it if that's what it is? And in the third place—and this is what I'm really interested in knowing about—what do I gain by beating around the bush with the guy, the way you're suggesting I do?"

"I've just told you, Buddy. You gain another day to think it over. That is, if he does meet you."

"But you still don't believe he meant what he said. Actually you don't believe he will show up, do you?"

She looked at him.

"Frankly, no," she said. "I don't. What makes you so certain he will?"

"The way he told me he would. But of course you won't go along with that, I realize that. The man's a criminal, as you say, so how can any law-abiding citizen take his word for anything?"

"Please, Buddy."

"Please *what?*" he demanded angrily.

She said nothing.

"O.K.," he said. "Tell you what we do. Let's make a bet on it."

"Oh, Buddy, stop being silly, please."

"What's silly about it? What's wrong with making a bet? What would you like to have if you win?"

She examined him for a few seconds.

"Are you really in earnest?" she asked then.

He nodded.

"Very well. Let me think about it." She cupped her chin in her hand. Presently she looked up. "All right, Buddy. I saw a string of small pearls in Cartier's window the other day. They're probably quite expensive. My grandmother used to have a string like that and I've always wanted one, since I was a little girl. Will that be suitable?"

"Fine," he said. "That'll do fine."

"Very well. What about you?"

"Never mind about me. I don't need anything."

"But that's not fair—that's no bet."

"What good's a bet between a husband and wife? I'm going to pay either way."

"Yes, I see," she said evenly. She gave him an odd look. "Supposing I were to pay if I lost?"

"I don't get it. Where would you get the money unless I gave it to you?"

"You seem to forget, Buddy. I used to earn my own living before we got married, or don't you remember? It was you who insisted I quit modeling—or wasn't it?"

"Ah, Marje, for God's sake, let's not go through all that again, shall we?"

"Yes, Buddy, I think we should," she said quietly.

"I'd really rather not," he said.

She shrugged. "Suit yourself, Buddy. It can wait. Perhaps you'll win your bet, in which case of course there won't be any need to discuss it." She was looking at him in that odd way again. "Will there?"

"Say, what's eating you, Marje?" he said. "What's going on all of a sudden? I don't get this. Will you please give me some idea of what's on your mind?"

"Why, certainly," she said. "You proposed a bet. I'm only trying to think of some way I'd be able to pay my end of the bet if I lose. That's all, there isn't any more."

"Oh, Marje, come on," he said.

After a moment she seemed to snap out of it, whatever it was. "All right, Buddy, let it go," she said. "But there is one more thing."

"What's that?" he said absently.

"I still think you should—" she began.

Just then he looked at the clock on the table beside the sofa where she was sitting.

"Say, it's eight-twenty," he said, jumping up. "I'm going to have to tear if I'm going to make it at all."

He went to the hall closet, got his hat and coat, and started toward the door.

She stood beside him. "Well, are you going to pay any attention to my suggestion?" she asked.

"Suggestion? What suggestion?"

"My suggestion about not having been able to raise the money—remember?"

He stood with his hand on the doorknob, trying to figure out what was in her mind. She looked blandly into his eyes.

"Look, Marje, I'll barely make it as it is. He said between eight-thirty and a quarter to nine. Can't we talk about it later?"

"It'll be too late then," she said. "Why not try it, Buddy? Leave part of the money with me. If he does come, tell him you'll have the rest of it tomorrow. Please, Buddy. I have a good reason for asking." Her eyes pleaded with him.

There was no time to think any further about it. He made a swift decision.

"O.K., Marje, have it your way." He took out the money, counted out four tens, and handed them to her. He let go of them reluctantly. "But suppose something goes wrong? Suppose he gets suspicious. Then I'll never get my watch back."

"You still don't know you're going to get it back anyway," she said. "Don't worry, dear. If he trusts you tonight there's no good reason why he won't trust you tomorrow night. If he doesn't come at all it won't make any difference anyway."

"But what'll I gain out of all this kibitzing around?" he said as he opened the door. "I don't get it, Marje."

"It's all right, dear. I'll explain later. Now run along—you don't want to be late for your—appointment, do you?"

He kissed her on the cheek and went out. While he waited for the elevator she stood in the doorway. "Oh, yes," she said, as the elevator arrived, "and while you're gone I'll try to figure out something to get you in case I lost our bet."

"Maybe you better find out the price of the pearls first," he said, grinning at her as the elevator door opened.

"Yes, that's a good idea. Goodbye, darling."

"Goodbye," he said, as she closed the door.

There were several men sitting at the bar when Buddy walked in. He looked around. The big man was nowhere in sight. He looked down the row of partitioned booths running along the wall opposite the bar. They were all empty. He took a stool at the bar and waited. A television set blared and the heads of the drinkers were all turned toward it. No one paid any attention to Buddy, including the fat bartender who stood off at the end of the bar staring up at the television screen. Buddy looked up and saw two colored boys mauling each other as a white-shirted referee danced around them in the flicker of the screen. "It's beginning to shape up to be a real scrap, friends," the unctuous voice of the announcer blatted. Now and then the hoarse roar of the crowd in the arena boomed over the speaker as one or the other of the fighters landed a punch.

Buddy watched the fight for a while, then turned away.

Well, he thought, here we are. Let's see what happens now.

He sat there, outwardly calm but inwardly bubbling with excitement and a curious sense of anticipation. "All right, now, take it easy," he kept telling himself. "It's early yet, he's still got almost ten minutes left to show up. He'll show up— of course he'll show up." Anyway, if he didn't . . .? In that case he'd be no worse off than he was before coming here. And perhaps he'd have learned something . . . Though what it was he would have learned he could not quite figure out.

He sat quietly for several minutes, keeping an eye on the entrance, hoping at any moment to see the big man walk in and at the same time trying to convince himself that he had no doubts.

"What's yours?" The fat bartender was standing across the bar, his pasty moon-face glistening sweatily.

"Scotch old-fashioned," Buddy told him. The bartender nodded curtly and waddled away. Buddy glanced back at the television screen. The two colored boys were now stretched out on small stools diagonally opposite each other across the ring. Men in sweatshirts hovered over them, rubbing them with towels, kneading them, and as Buddy stared absently up at the screen the scene dissolved into a picture of an immense beer glass. A new announcer's voice began an interminable spiel. "Friends, have you ever tried . . ." Buddy turned away, mentally tuning out the commercial.

The bartender was back now and his drink stood on the wood before him. He picked it up, took a sip, and watched the bartender waddle back to the end of the bar. He took another sip and just then he felt a light tap on his shoulder. He looked up and saw the big man standing there, his face expressionless, his eyes on Buddy's.

"Hi," Buddy said uncertainly.

"How they going?" the man said.

"Have a drink?"

The man took the stool next to Buddy's.

"O.K.," he said. "Don't mind if I do."

Buddy signalled the bartender, who waddled over, took the order, and went away.

"You got the dough on you?"

"Yes," Buddy said, trying to sound quite casual, "that is . . ."

The man looked narrowly at him. "That is what?"

Buddy waited till the bartender brought a shot glass of straight rye, put it down in front of the man, and left, before he answered.

"I couldn't get hold of the whole hundred today," he said, not looking directly at his companion.

The big fellow ignored the drink before him, gave Buddy a swift, suspicious glance, then made as if to get up.

"Hold it a minute, can't you?" Buddy said hastily. "All I could raise was sixty dollars. I brought it along anyway, to show you I meant what I said last night," turning to look up at the other.

The man sat back down.

"What'd you have in mind, Mac?"

"Well . . . I was sort of hoping you'd be willing to let me have another day. Either that or let me have the watch for the sixty dollars."

The man said nothing, just watched Buddy.

"Of course," Buddy added, "if you can't see your way to that I'll be glad to give you the whole hundred, as I said last night. I know I can have it by tomorrow."

The man looked away, his fingers drumming softly on the bar. At last he turned back to Buddy.

"Look, Mac," he said. "Way I figure it, we made a deal. You said a hundred, and a hundred's what I'll take."

Buddy took a sip of his drink. "Yes, I can see your point of view," he said gravely. "What do you suggest?"

"You sure you can get the dough tomorrow?"

"Positive," said Buddy.

The big fellow hesitated. "O.K.," he said. "I guess that'll be O.K." He gulped down the rye and started to get up. "See you here tomorrow."

"What's your hurry?" Buddy said.

The other shrugged. "No special hurry," he said. "I just figured we were finished with our business and I—"

"May as well have one more for the road."

The man pursed his lips, then grinned embarrassedly. "Sure, might as well. O.K."

When the bartender brought them their drinks Buddy picked up his glass, turned to the big fellow, and said, "Cheers."

"Here's to you," the man said politely, holding up his shot glass.

They drank.

"You know?" Buddy said as he put his glass down on the bar. "I half expected you wouldn't even show up tonight."

The man laughed shortly. "Tell you the truth, Mac, you were about half right. I damn near didn't."

"Thought I might try to pull a fast one, is that it?"

"Well, you know how it is." He shrugged and looked down into his empty shot glass. "Put yourself in my place. How would I know what you might've figured out since last night?"

"Yes, of course . . . But you decided to come along anyway. So you must have figured you could take my word. Right?"

He gave Buddy an enigmatic look, shrugged again, then said, "Want me to level with you?"

"Why not?"

"Tell you how I figured it," the man said. "First place, you sounded like you really meant it when you were saying about the watch and all."

Buddy nodded.

"But that wasn't the whole thing," the man went on, "because later on, after I left you there, I got to thinking over the angles. First thing I figured was, you might have meant everything, just like you said, but still and all by the time tonight came around you could've got to talking to somebody or else thought about it some more and figured you might as well save yourself a hundred bucks. What the hell, it's only human nature."

Buddy sat quietly, secretly amused at the accuracy of all this.

"So at first I thought the hell with it, why stick my neck out? But then I got to thinking about what you said about the watch being something your old man gave you."

The man paused, took out a pack of cigarettes, offered one to Buddy. After they had both lit up, he went on. "And then I got to thinking about that and . . ." here he broke into a sheepish grin, "from there I got to thinking about the hundred bucks. . . ." He stopped and gazed thoughtfully at the bar mirror. "What the hell, no sense me trying to kid you, Mac. I can use the dough. You can figure that out for yourself, I guess, after last night."

Buddy nodded, took a puff of his cigarette, and said, "Yes . . . Go ahead, though. I'm sort of curious to hear the rest of it."

"Well, I finally figured I might as well come by and see what'd happen," the man said. "But still, I wasn't too sure what you might've decided since last night, see? So what I did, I got here earlier and hung around across the way till I saw you come in here by yourself. Then I waited a few more minutes to make sure."

"I see. You wanted to make sure I wasn't going to try anything before you stuck your neck out all the way. Right?"

The man seemed to weigh Buddy's question for a while. At length he nodded and said, "Yeah, I guess you could say that. But I don't know as you can blame me for being a little careful. Know what I mean?"

"Of course," Buddy said. "But as long as you're being so careful, doesn't it occur to you that I could have been careful too?"

The big man exhaled a cloud of smoke and peered at Buddy through it.

"I don't think I follow you there, Mac," he said evenly.

"Let me explain," Buddy said, beginning to enjoy the situation. "After all, what was there to prevent me from planting someone at the bar here, before I came here myself—" letting his eyes flick across the other drinkers ranged along the bar, "and then wait for you to show up before turning you in?" He watched the man's eyes closely as he went on, "As, for instance, I could do right this moment—that is, if I had really planted someone here, which, by the way, I didn't, just in case you're interested."

Throughout all this, the man simply sat there regarding him expressionlessly.

"Yeah," he said, speaking slowly, "that's something else I thought about." Somehow Buddy got the impression that he was amused.

"Well, how did you know I wouldn't do it?"

"Tell you the God's honest truth, Mac," the big man suddenly laughed, "I didn't know. But I kinda figured you wouldn't. . . . See?" drawing out Buddy's watch and displaying it. "I even brought along the evidence, that's how sure I was."

Buddy looked down at the watch. "Yes, I see," he said, feeling a bit foolish.

"Well," the man said, replacing the watch in his pocket, "I guess that's about it. Now, about tomorrow night. . . ."

After making an appointment for the following evening they started out. On the way Buddy reached into his pocket and held the six ten-dollar bills in his hand. When they reached the sidewalk he took the money out and held it toward the man.

"What's that for?" the man said.

"Here, take it," Buddy said. "You might as well hold it till tomorrow night."

The big fellow slowly reached out for the bills. He held them in his hand.

"I don't know," he said uncertainly. "I guess it's O.K.," looking into Buddy's eyes. He grinned crookedly and suddenly asked, "Why don't you hang onto it yourself, Mac? Till you get the rest of it."

"It's no use to me," Buddy said. "And this way you have proof that I'll meet you tomorrow."

"It wouldn't just happen to be marked, would it?"

"Say, what do you think I am?" Buddy asked indignantly.

"Ah, I was only kidding you," the man said.

"Well," Buddy said sarcastically, "no sense taking my word for anything. Take a good look at it later on, just in case."

"Listen, Mac, no use getting sore. Maybe I will at that. You know how it is. Fellow in my position can't take too many chances."

"You still don't trust me," Buddy said. "Seriously—you don't, do you?"

The man stopped grinning.

"Tell you the truth, Mac, I don't really know. Been a while since I trusted anybody. I guess maybe I *kinda* trust you but still. . . ."

"But still, no sense taking unnecessary risks, that it?"

The man said nothing.

"Well, look it over real carefully," Buddy said. "Play it real safe. Hell, I wouldn't want you losing any sleep over this."

"I don't know what you're so sore about, Mac," the man said. "What the hell, I was here with the watch like I said, wasn't I?"

"Yes, and so was I here," Buddy answered. "After all, I'm taking a certain risk myself, wouldn't you say?"

"Risk? How do you mean, risk?"

"You've now got sixty dollars of my money as a—as a sort of retainer, haven't you? What guarantee have I got that you won't just take it and never show up again? Wouldn't that indicate a certain amount of trust I'm placing on your word?"

The man stood quietly for a few seconds. "Yeah, I guess you got something there, at that," he finally answered. "But don't worry about it, I'll show up."

"That's not the point," Buddy said. "The thing is, I *am* trusting you."

"Look, Mac, I don't know what you expect me to say. All I can tell you is I'll be here. That's that. If you got any doubts about it, here—take it, it's still your dough."

"No, never mind," Buddy said, ignoring the money. "Keep it, it's yours. I'll take your word."

"I'm taking yours," the man said. "You can take mine."

Buddy watched him put the money into his pocket.

"Would you like to know why I'm giving it to you to-night?"

The man waited for him to go on.

"It's because you took a chance with me tonight," Buddy said. "The plain truth is, I never expected to see either you or my watch again. In fact, I even made a bet with some-one."

Abruptly the man grinned at him. "Well, I'm sorry you lost your bet."

"Lost it?" Buddy said. "Oh no—I won."

"Won? I thought you said you bet on me not showing."

"No, I bet you would show up. You see, I was sort of trying to make myself believe you would, probably because I was practically convinced you wouldn't."

"Sounds kinda mixed up," the man said.

"I suppose it is pretty mixed up," Buddy answered. "Any-way, I'm glad I won. Not only because of the bet and not even because of the watch, actually. . . . But that's why I'm giving you the money tonight, to show you I am taking your word that you'll be here tomorrow night. Do you understand that?"

The big man examined Buddy gravely for a few seconds.

"Maybe," he said. "I don't know for sure. . . . Anyhow I'll be here."

Buddy stuck out his hand. The man took it, gripped it, then walked away. Buddy stood looking after him until he disappeared.

On his way home Buddy felt such a jubilant sense of vindication that he decided to play a joke on Marjorie. Actually, he told himself, it was not so much a joke on her as a nice way of showing her how mistaken she had been.

"Well?" she asked, as he walked in.

"Well nothing," he said, pulling a long face. "You win. Go on down and get the string of pearls tomorrow."

She looked at him for a moment, and a sort of smug, righteous look came over her face.

"I'm sorry, Buddy," she said. "Truly I am. I don't really want the pearls, it was only because you insisted."

"No, you've got to get them," he said. "You won. A bet's a bet."

They argued about it for a little while. In the end she agreed to pick up the pearls the next day.

In the morning, as he was leaving Marjorie said, "Oh, by the way, you may as well take this forty dollars back. I've still got some money in my account."

"O.K.," he said, casually taking the four ten-dollar bills. "I've still got the sixty from last night but I suppose I may as well take this, long as you don't need it."

That evening when he came home Marjorie was wearing the pearls.

"Look, darling," she said, "aren't they the most beautiful things you ever laid eyes on?"

"No," he said, looking gravely at her face. "They're not."

She looked hurt.

"Oh, Buddy, I thought you'd love them. What's wrong with them? Don't you like them?"

"I like 'em all right," he said. "But they're not the most beautiful things I've ever seen . . . You are, though."

She laughed and threw her arms around him.

"Oh, Buddy. Darling, I love you so much."

"That's fine, Marje," he said, "because I love you even more than that."

He made an excuse to leave at about eight-fifteen and took a cab to Ryan's Bar and Grill. He was quite excited at the prospect of meeting the man and getting his watch back so he could come home and show it to Marjorie. He had it all worked out that he would walk back into the apartment, sit down as if nothing had happened, and then sometime during the evening nonchalantly pull out his watch and announce the time. He wanted to see her face when she realized how he had fooled her. And now, with the pearls and everything, he felt pretty set-up about the whole thing.

This time, when he walked into the saloon, he saw the big fellow at the bar waiting for him. Buddy went over to him.

"Hi there," he said.

The man looked up from his glass of beer.

"How's it going?" he said.

"I've got the money," Buddy said. "You've got the watch, haven't you?"

"Sure," the man answered, reaching into his pocket and drawing it out.

Buddy took out the four tens, handed them over, took his watch, and looked at it fondly.

"Well," he said, "that about straightens us out, doesn't it?"

"Just about," the man answered.

The fat bartender waddled over.

"Care for a drink?" Buddy asked.

The man shrugged.

"Guess I could stand a shot of rye," he said.

Buddy ordered an old-fashioned for himself. When the drinks were set down before them, Buddy raised his glass.

"Here's luck," he said.

The big fellow raised his shot glass and nodded.

"Luck to *you*," he said, taking a sip of his rye and then a gulp of beer.

Buddy had just put his drink down when he saw a stocky man in a badly-cut grey suit come in, stand in the doorway, and look around. After a moment the man's eyes came to rest on him and he raised his eyebrows. Buddy had no idea who it could be and he started to turn away. Then he saw the man come toward him.

"You Mr. Ross?" the stocky man said.

"Why, yes, but I don't think I—"

He had no time to finish the sentence. All at once a number of things took place in rapid succession.

To his amazement his companion suddenly turned and shot him a look of undiluted hatred. At the same instant the stocky man laid a beefy hand on the big fellow's shoulder and pushed him back down as he started to get up from his stool.

The big man turned to the newcomer. "What's this all about?" he asked flatly, his face hard and set.

The stocky man reached into his hip pocket and brought out a battered wallet, flipped it open to display a police badge, then returned it to his pocket.

"O.K., Buster," he said, ignoring Buddy. "Way I got the story, you pulled a little stick-up the other night and got some money and a watch."

"But I don't get it," Buddy finally managed to say.

Neither of the men paid him any attention.

"Come on," the detective said, "le'me see what you got in your pockets, Buster." He smiled frostily, still ignoring Buddy completely.

"Listen, officer," Buddy said, laying his hand on the detective's arm, "I think you've made some mistake. This man is a friend of mine. Here's my watch," pulling it out and showing it to the detective, who now began to look puzzled.

"What the hell's goin' on here, mister?" he asked, looking from Buddy to the big man and back to Buddy again. "I just

got orders to come down here and look for a Mr. Ross—
that's you, isn't it?—and pick up a fella who stuck you up
the other night and took your watch away."

"But I've *got* my watch," Buddy said. "Here it is."

The bartender was standing by, watching curiously. Now
Buddy noticed a policeman standing in the doorway, looking
over. The big man was looking at Buddy with a strange
expression on his face. The detective looked down at the
watch in Buddy's hand, from that to Buddy's face, then back
to the big man. He rubbed his chin.

"I'll be goddamned if this isn't a—" Abruptly turning back
to Buddy, "Look, you *are* Mr. Ross, right?" he asked.

"Why, yes, I am," Buddy said, "but I don't see—"

"Never mind," the detective said. "Listen, you," turning
back to the big fellow. "Le'me see what you got in your
pockets."

The big man looked at him, then at Buddy, then back to
the detective again. "You heard Mr. Ross, didn't you?" he
said. "Didn't he just get through telling you you must've
made some mistake? You saw his watch, didn't you?"

"Yeah, yeah, never mind all that," the detective said impatiently. "Come on, let's see what you got on you. Or do
you want to play games?" He looked meaningfully toward
the policeman but shook his head from side to side as the
policeman started to come forward.

The big fellow glanced over his shoulder, saw the policeman, shrugged, put his hand in his pocket, and brought out
the money Buddy had just handed him. The detective took
the four bills and reached into his own pocket for a slip of
paper. He compared the bills with the slip of paper, looking
carefully at the serial numbers on the ten dollar bills, then
slipped the bills and the paper into his pocket.

"All right, Buster, I think this oughta do it," he said to the
big fellow. "Come on, looks like you're goin' away for a
while."

The big man's expression underwent a curious transformation. He seemed not to have heard the detective. His eyes were right on Buddy's and there was a look in them that made Buddy squirm.

"Look," Buddy told him earnestly, "I tell you I had nothing to do with this. I don't know any more about it than—" But even as he said it he knew he did know.

The big man's eyes turned away as he got slowly to his feet. Suddenly the detective reached into his coat pocket, pulled out a pair of handcuffs, and clamped them on the big fellow's wrists. Now the policeman came forward. Buddy looked on helplessly. There was a sinking sensation in the pit of his stomach. In another moment the detective, the policeman and the big man were gone.

"What the hell happened?"

Buddy looked up and saw the bartender.

"Nothing much," Buddy answered. He mumbled something about a hold-up and all at once he wanted to get out of there. A few men down the bar were staring over. He took out a couple of bills, laid them on the bar, and went out . . .

"Just a moment, please," Marjorie was saying as he came into his apartment. She was speaking into the telephone, facing him as he walked in. "Here's Mr. Ross now," cupping her hand over the mouthpiece of the instrument and whispering, "It's the police, Buddy. They've just brought him in and they want to talk to you."

He gave her a long look.

"Talk to them yourself," he said. "It was your idea. Talk to them yourself."

He took off his hat and coat, hung them in the hall closet, came into the living room and began fixing himself a stiff drink.

"I'm sorry, I made a mistake," Marjorie said into the telephone. "It wasn't Mr. Ross after all." Her eyes were fixed on Buddy as she spoke. "No, I really can't say but he should be here any moment . . . You say you'll need someone to lodge a formal complaint?" Her eyes signalled Buddy but he looked away. "Yes, of course. I'll tell him the moment he arrives. Yes . . . Yes, I'll have him call you immediately. . . . Very well. Goodbye."

She hung up and came over to him. He looked pointedly down into his drink and sat down.

There was a tense silence. He could feel her standing there, looking at him, but he stared doggedly down at his glass.

"Buddy," she said at last. "Please, darling, I only did what I thought was right."

He said nothing.

"Was it so wrong of me?" she pleaded.

"What about what *I* thought was right?" Buddy suddenly shouted, glaring up at her. "Don't *I* have any right to an opinion about what's right?"

She crouched down beside him.

"Please, Buddy, let me explain. I think you'll understand if you'll only let me explain."

"There's only one thing I'd be interested in having you explain," he said. "How did you know? How did you *know?*"

She said nothing for a moment.

"How the hell did you *know,* for Christ's sake?" he shouted.

"Please, Buddy, calm yourself," she said.

"Never mind about that," he shouted. "Tell me, will you, for the love of Jesus? *How the hell did you know?*"

She stood up.

"Very well. I'll tell you." She went to the sofa and sat down, drawing her legs up under her. "There's really nothing so terribly clever about it. You're probably the most unskillful liar in the world, do you know that, Buddy?"

He said nothing at all, just sat there staring across the room at her. She was undoubtedly lovely and just then he noticed that she was wearing the string of pearls but the only thing he wanted to do was to get up, walk over there, and slap her, hard, right across her lovely face. He did nothing though, simply sat looking at her.

"Actually," she went on smugly, "I suppose I half knew it immediately when you walked in last night. There was a—a kind of look about you, a sort of self-satisfied look. I know that look of yours, Buddy. After all, I've seen it before."

"Never mind my look," he said. "Go on."

"Well . . ." she said. "I think I guessed it right then. But naturally I couldn't be sure. Then when you told me to go get the pearls—well, then I began to wonder. But there was still no way to know for certain, not until after you'd gone to sleep."

"What did my going to sleep have to do with anything?"

"That was the first time I had an opportunity to find out whether you still had the sixty dollars, don't you see?"

"You mean you played wifey and went through my pockets, that it?"

She nodded. She was trying to remain serious, so as not to offend him, but now a tiny smile played on her lips.

"Was that so terribly naughty of me?" she asked, making fun of the word naughty, stressing it comically, as she gave him an arch look.

"Never mind—go on," he said.

"Well, when I saw you didn't have the six ten-dollar bills, I began to get suspicious. But I still couldn't be certain. Until this morning, when you said you still had the sixty dollars, and of course then I knew you were trying to play a trick on me. It took me a little while to figure out just what you were up to but after a few minutes I saw through it all right. You had decided to go through with your—your little deal with that man and then show me how wrong I'd been. Wasn't that it? Tell the truth, Buddy, wasn't it?"

"That's close enough," he said sourly. "But go on, what happened then?"

"Well, as soon as I had thought all that out I decided I'd play a joke on *you*. So I went and picked up the pearls, to make you think I believed you had lost the bet. But don't worry, dear, I haven't paid for them. I can return them tomorrow. I only wanted to fool you."

"Yes, I see. And then?"

"Oh, the rest was simple enough. I knew where you were to meet the man. Or at least I assumed you'd be meeting him at the same place you told me yesterday—so I called the police and told them about it. I also gave them the serial numbers of the four ten-dollar bills. I copied them off before I gave them back to you. And that's all there was to it. Nothing so terribly clever about it after all, was there?"

She was laughing at him now, looking over at him as if she expected him to laugh too. He sat there staring steadily at her, his face grim, and gradually she stopped laughing, stopped smiling, and looked at him in puzzlement.

"What's the trouble, Buddy?"

"Nothing," he said, shaking his head. "You handled it perfectly. I'm proud of you."

Her eyebrows raised.

"Yep, I'm real proud of you, Marje. You did a noble thing tonight, put a criminal behind bars where he belongs. Tell me, how's it feel to know you did right, does it feel good?"

"Buddy, what's the matter with you? You're behaving so—I've never seen you like this. What is it?"

"You really want to know?" he asked, looking at her with hate in his eyes.

She stared at him and nodded slowly. He got up, walked deliberately across the room with his drink in his hand, and without warning threw the contents of the glass, ice and all, into her face. She sat perfectly still for a moment, looking up at him with a stunned expression, then slowly began wiping her face with one hand. She was shaking her head just the least bit from side to side and she went on wiping her face dazedly. Her eyes had a stricken look in them and she never took them from his.

"*That's* the way I feel about it," he said, stiff-lipped, eyeing her coldly. Then he looked down, saw the glass in his hand, and hurled it against the wall with all the strength he had, watching with a sort of satisfaction as the fragments scattered over the carpet.

This time she shrank away from him, her eyes fixed on his face as if he had been suddenly transformed into some loathsome creature.

"That too," he said, looking back at her. "*That's* the way I feel too. I hope you're pleased. You've done a fine night's work."

He turned and stormed out of the living room, into the bedroom, sat down on the edge of the bed, and held his face in his hands. There was no sound from the other room.

He had no idea how long he remained there in the dark, but finally he got up and went back into the living room. Marjorie was sitting right where he had left her, her expression blank, her face wooden-looking. She stared off into space and even after he had come in and sat down again she still went on staring off into space with a frozen, dead look in her eyes . . .

"And that was that," Buddy concluded, looking off into space himself.

"What happened after that?" I asked, staring at him in astonishment. "What did she do? You don't mean to say that was the end of it, do you?"

He nodded.

"Sure, that was it. Next day she left. We were divorced a few months later. But that was really the end of it, that night. This is the first time I've even laid eyes on her since the divorce."

He looked at me oddly, then broke into a crooked little grin, and said, "Did you notice something, Fred? The pearls she had on . . ."

"She kept them?" I asked incredulously.

"Oh, I insisted on it," he said. "Hell, it seemed to me she deserved them. Sort of a memento."

I said nothing.

"Well? What do you think?" he now asked. "Kind of weird, isn't it?"

"Yes," I said, "it's kind of weird all right."

His next words seemed to come right out of left field, or some other improbable place.

"Say, Fred," he said, "did you ever stop to think that maybe when Eve handed Adam the apple she was really doing him a favor?"

"What the hell have Adam and Eve got to do with it?" I asked.

"And that maybe the apple didn't come from the tree of knowledge at all?" he went on, as if he hadn't even heard me. "Seems to me, from what I can see of the whole damn human race, she must have got the apple from some altogether different tree. The tree of stupidity, maybe. Seems to me we could all use an apple from the tree of knowledge, don't you think? Or maybe that damn snake knew just what he was up to all the time. . . ."

"I don't think I quite follow you, Buddy," I said. "I've got a sort of small flash but I don't believe I've picked up the whole message."

"Oh, hell," he said. "Too complicated, probably. Maybe nobody ever gets anybody else's whole message. Anyway, think about it, Fred. I think you'll get more and more of it as time goes on. That is if you feel like thinking about it."

"Sure, Buddy, I'll think about it once in a while," I said, smiling at him.

"Wonder what time it is," he said pulling out his heavy gold pocket watch. "My God! Three-twenty-five. I've got to get going."

"Me too," I said.

He started to signal for the waiter to bring us our check.

"Is that the watch?" I asked.

"The watch?" he asked. "Oh, yes—that's it."

"And the big guy? Did you ever see him again?"

"Oh yes," he grinned wryly. "I was forced to testify against him."

"Forced?"

"Yes. After they subpoenaed me, I had no choice. I had to appear, and I couldn't quite bring myself to commit perjury."

"But why?" I persisted. "I mean, why would they have gone to such lengths if you wanted to drop the matter?"

"Oh, well." Buddy shrugged. "They couldn't very well let it go—not with all the pressure being brought to bear on them, don't you see?" He looked toward the corner of the restaurant, where Marjorie and her friend were still sitting.

"Pressure—you mean from her?" I said, glancing over there myself.

"Naturally," he said. "Why not? She seemed to feel pretty strongly about it, so why not?"

"Yes, I suppose so," I said. "But still . . ."

"Still what?"

"Nothing, Buddy. I suppose there really isn't anything to say, is there?"

"No, Fred," he said. "I guess not."

"Well," I said lightly. "Sure is enough to make a fellow stop and think."

He laughed and signalled for the waiter to bring the check.

"Sure is," he grinned. "Bet your boots and all that. I might even add, you can say that again, old-timer."

"Go on, add it," I said.

"All right," he laughed. "You can say that again, old-timer."

"O.K., Buddy," I said. "Sure is enough to make a fellow stop and think."

We were both grinning as the waiter came over but I had a strong suspicion that neither of us thought it was as funny as all that.

Old Friend

Old Friend

1

You've heard of Steve Larsen, haven't you? Guess pretty near everybody has by now, except I suppose most people don't know him as Steve, only his friends—name he writes under is Stephen, Stephen A. Larsen. I never did know what the A. stands for and now I probably never will unless I find out from somebody else besides him. Cause I'm pretty sure I won't be seeing much of Steve anymore, not after what happened.

In a way I'm kinda sorry it ever happened. Like if I'd of never found out about him we'd probably still be pals. And I'll tell you this much right off, I'm gonna miss the guy, know what I mean? Cause I sure dug him the most. We always used to have plenty of laughs whenever we got together, on account of he's got this real mad sense of humor and whenever he was around it just seemed like everything got wild and like not for real.

Come to think about it it's kinda funny a guy like Steve should of ever become a poet. Like I always figured poets to be long-hair types with horn rim cheaters and all like that. At least I always used to before I run into Steve.

Fact first time I met him I couldn't hardly believe he was a poet at all, not even after he told me so himself. Like I figured somebody was trying to put me on.

Course back in those days—this is about nineteen thirty-five, thirty-six, around in there—you couldn't hardly say he made much of a living at it. Like I remember how kinda raggedy he looked first time I ever saw him and he had on this old beatup suit looked like it might of belonged to some hobo. Newspaper guy I used to know around Chicago name of Joe Carney brought Steve over to this brokendown joint I was singing in, told me this guy's kinda like a fan of mine—you know, from hearing me on some of them old records I used to do vocals on. Like with that Natchez bunch, the watchamacallems, the Natchez Hot Five—or them New Orleans Washboard Blue Blowers, remember them old-time jazz records? Some of 'em become what they call collectors items now, hear you gotta lay out ten or fifteen clams to get ahold of one of 'em nowadays, how *about* that? Sounds to me like these collector characters are a lot of flips, if you know what I mean.

But anyhow. At first I was gonna give this raggedy-looking character the old brush even if Joe Carney does tell me he's a real poet. What the hell—who's looking for a poet? But soon's Steve starts talking it up a little in between shows I kinda change my mind. And by the time we had a few snorts and one thing and another, the guy's got me laughing fit to split a gut. He was one of the wildest-talking characters I ever run into and believe me, man, a guy singing around the kinda joints I used to work in gets to hear plenty of wild dialogue, know what I mean? Thing about Steve though, he wasn't only a wild talker—cause all the time he was saying some of these mad things'd really knock you out, still and all it was like underneath everything he was making more sense'n anybody you ever met in your life.

Well, after that first time Joe Carney brought him by Steve come back by himself a few more times. Like he'd fall in the joint every once in a while and we'd have a few fast ones at the bar and after a couple weeks or so we got to be pretty good friends. Steve was born and raised right there in Chicago and he knew the town real good. Also seemed like everybody knew him too. Like I remember I used to finish up my last show in that little trap down there on the South Side and then me'n Steve'd start out together and before I finally fell into my pad next morning we'd of been in some of the wildest little traps you ever seen. He used to write about these weird cats we'd see right there in these little traps where they used to hang out night after night juicing it up or blowing pot or even on the real righteous stuff some of 'em—you know, Horse or some of 'em goofed up on Charlie, like they used to call it. Steve used to talk to 'em by the hour. Talk about wild-talking characters! But Steve wrote a lot of it down and anybody's picked up on his stuff knows what I'm driving at all right.

Anyhow by the time I finished up that gig and left Chicago Steve and me were real pals. Later on after his first book come out and became a big hit he made some pretty good cabbage out of selling the picture rights and then he came on to New York and we got together again. By that time I was starting to do okay too. Like I'd just scored pretty big doing a single in the Paramount and from there I went into the Copa and did all right there and about that time I made a couple new records and those hit big and then, well, you know how it is in my racket. Pretty soon I signed a deal to make a picture at Metro and it looked like yours truly was finally up in the chips and everything was real cool.

Meantime Steve got out another one of them nutty books of his and this one did even better'n the first one. First thing you know he's becoming kind of a cockeyed big shot—like a celebrity around the book racket. I guess maybe it was partly on account of most people in that racket didn't know what the hell to make of a guy like Steve. Like I told you, he looks more like a bum than a writer. I mean *you* know, he's long and tall and skinny and kinda hungry-looking and he never has learned how to dress and all like that. He still wears these corny suits made out of some kinda tweed, and I guess he must hate barbers like poison cause I never see the guy when he didn't look like he just got back from a long trip through a jungle or something. Frankly, you want to know what I really think, I think the guy must cut his own goddamn hair cause honest to God, man, I can't see how the hell anybody can keep on looking like that without he works kinda hard at it, dig?

But anyhow, he kept taking things nice and cool even after people started making like a fuss over him and we got to be real good pals over the next ten, eleven years or so. Course once I got up into the big cabbage I had to do a certain amount of touring around the country and then I went out the coast and made that first picture for Metro and it did real great at the box office so next thing you know they're after me to sign a deal to make five more, one a year, and with all that happening I kept kinda on the go, dig? But still and all in between times I'd get back to the Apple and whenever I got to town I used to get together with old Steve and we'd cut up a few touches for old times sake. I guess you might say we were like old buddies by that time and I'm sure we'd of stayed that way for the rest of our lives if this thing hadn't of happened.

All I gotta say is I never been so fooled about a guy in my whole life. Like I still don't hardly know what to believe— except of course I got the dope right out of his own wife's mouth. I know it's got to be true, cause nobody could make up something like this and tell it the way she told me, not even if they were the best actress in the world, which Betsy Larsen is not even an actress at all. But even after she told me about it and I gave it to Steve straight out even *then* he still wouldn't admit it. Course, point is Steve can talk up a real storm. I've heard him go and I know he's the kinda guy can take any side in any argument and pretty damn near every time wind up in front, know what I mean? I suppose a guy writes for a living gets so after a while he can make words do damn near anything he wants 'em to do. Fact come to think about it I just remembered Steve himself telling me one time that more people use words to cover *up* the truth than to tell it. Or something like that anyhow, cause I don't remember exactly *how* he said it—but now I guess I dig what he was driving at all right.

But let me give you the whole thing just like it happened. First I gotta go back quite a ways on account of this started out like around thirty-nine, forty, when I was out the coast that first trip. That was when I met Betsy Larsen—only naturally her name wasn't Larsen then . . .

2

I guess I must of been kinda mixed up around that time—you know, Hollywood and all—or else things probably wouldn't of happened like they did. After all, I mean, I was nothing but a plain beatup saloon singer, you understand, and here I was now all of a sudden making more bread in just one week than I'd ever seen in my whole life. I must of gone a little haywire with it all. First thing, I bought me a nutty robins-egg-blue Caddy convertible, real sharp. Then I went and rented me a great big house on top of a hill, with a swimming pool and a crazy big bar—and all kinds of groovey stuff like that. What the hell. In those days I wouldn't of known a surtax from a fingerbowl.

So, one day there was this big bunch of people up at my house and there's this one wild-looking little chick came along with some people, I don't remember who now but I think I remember somebody telling me she went to school with somebody's daughter, or something like that. Anyhow she was awful young. But she wasn't all *that* young, like I found out later on that afternoon when everybody put on bathing suits. We were all hanging around the pool having drinks and kibitzing around and all like that when here comes this little chick all dressed up in about three and a half square inches of damn near skin-colored cloth. Period. I'm telling you, man, my eyes must of bugged out a mile. And I wasn't the only one, man. Cause this chick really *had* it—I mean *all* of it and maybe even a little left over and spread around in the right places too. Then after she hopped into the pool and swam around a little this bathing suit of hers—if you wanna call it that—was sticking to her body like it was her own skin and believe me, it was enough to drive a man out of his skull to just *look* at her. On top of everything else she had this kinda baby face, all fulla freckles and real innocent-looking, and I guess that might of had more to do with it than anything else—as if the rest of it wasn't enough! Look—I don't mean to go on and on like this cause maybe it seems like I'm trying to make a whole big thing out of nothing but a little broad, you understand, but still and all, this chick was really *stacked,* man! There was quite a few other good-looking chicks around that pool that day, plenty of 'em doing all right for themselves in pictures, where it don't exactly hurt a broad to be stacked, dig? But all I can tell you is this little baby-faced chick with that innocent-looking kisser all full of freckles was making the rest of them pros look like a bunch of St. Bernards.

I was trying to make out like I wasn't paying her no mind but at the same time I couldn't keep my eyes off her—I'm telling you, she was the bitter *end,* man!

Finally I couldn't stand it any more so I got ahold of Sammy Green. Sammy used to be my agent out there and he knew pretty near everybody and everybody's business. I took him into a corner and asked him who the hell *is* this little chick and what does a guy have to do to get next to *that* for the love of God!

"Her name is Betsy Huntington," Sammy told me. "Her old man is loaded. He's Benjamin J. Huntington of—"

"Who cares about her old man, for Chri'sake?" I butted in. "All I'm askin', who *is* she?"

"I'm tryin' to tell you," he said. "She's one o' those debutantes. Cute little number, huh?"

"Cute?" I said, looking over at her. "Whooo-eeee! I'm gonna go'n' pick up on some o' that debutante deal right now."

And I started to go right over and see what kinda time I could make. But Sammy grabs me.

"Listen, Billy," he says. "Take my advice and be a smart boy. Lay off. She's jail bait."

"I didn't ask you how old she is, Sammy," I told him.

"Okay, Billy," he says, giving me one of them looks. "But don't say I didn't try to warn you. I happen to know she's only seventeen so if you wanna make a pass it's your funeral."

"Yeah, I heard you, Sammy," I told him. "Thanks for the advice and all. Only I happen to be one o' them guys enjoys funerals."

"Okay, sweetheart," he says. "I guess it's no use tryin' to make sense when a guy gets that look in his eye like you got. So c'mon over—I'll interduce you myself." That Sammy Green. What a character.

So he takes me over and interduces me and then he gets lost and I talk to her for a little while. Turns out she's only gonna be in Hollywood a couple more weeks and then she's going back to New York. She and her old lady—only she called her Mother, sounded real classy the way she said it— anyhow, she and the old lady were only out here like on a visit. And we go on talking about this and that and the more I talk to her the more I wanna see of her. (I guess that last remark just kinda slipped out like, but I might as well leave it stand that way.)

But still and all I had a hunch it wouldn't be such a smart idea to start rushing things with this chick. Cause innocent-looking or not she didn't act like no kid who didn't know the score. Also she didn't talk like no seventeen either. Like I could kinda tell she was letting me know she'd been around enough so she knew I wasn't only interested in conversation with her, dig? And jail bait or no jail bait I could see she didn't mind me feeling that way about her. You can pretty near always tell. *You* know. I guess maybe it's something in how they look at you. Anyhow, I could tell she kinda had eyes too, by how she was acting.

Course I had no idea where the hell it could go from here on account of she also mentioned how her old lady was pretty strict and didn't like for her to be running around much. But still and all I had hopes we might be able to figure out something, so I asked if maybe she'd like to come out to the studio with me and have a look around, one of these days.

"Oh, that would be marvelous, Mr. Miles," she said, looking up at me with them crazy baby-blues of hers. "I'd love that and I'm sure Mother wouldn't object."

"Fine, all you gotta do is say when," I said, "and I'm your boy. And by the way, the name is Billy."

"All right," she said, looking down, "—Billy."

"That's better," I said. "But you still didn't say when, honey."

"Why, almost any afternoon would be lovely," she said.

"Okay, no sense wastin' time then," I said, grinning at her. "How's about tomorrow?"

"Tomorrow would be marvelous," she said.

She looked up at me and smiled. She had these tiny little white teeth and no lipstick and, well, if it hadn't of been for all them other cats around, I don't know what I'd of done to her right then and there. Anyhow, she must of got the general drift from how I was staring down at her—she was only a little bit of a thing, hardly came up to my shoulders—cause I sure as hell wasn't trying to hide how I felt.

She looked away and said something.

"What'd you say, honey?" I asked her.

"I said tomorrow will be lovely," she said.

"Oh—oh yeah, tomorrow," I said. "Guess I wasn't listenin', honey."

"I guess you weren't, Billy," she said and all of a sudden we both bust out laughing.

When we quit laughing I asked her where I could call her. But she said it would be better if she called me. So I gave her my phone number. I was gonna write it on a piece of paper but she told me never mind, she could remember it okay. And that was it.

Next day by about noon I was sure she'd forgot the number and I was just beginning to kick myself all over the joint for not writing it down and giving it to her cause I figured now I'd probably never see her again and then all of a sudden the phone went off and I grabbed it. Sure enough it was Betsy all right.

Right after lunch I picked her up and we went out to the studio and spent the afternoon visiting the different sets where they were shooting—my picture was already in the can and I was just hanging around town having myself like a little vacation before going out on tour again.

So anyhow, by the time me and Betsy left the studio I had such a yen for her I couldn't hardly control myself. But like I said before, I had this hunch she wasn't the kind of a chick it would be a good idea to try to crowd her. So I played it real cool and everything was nice and polite and all like that and finally I drove her back home. Only when we were saying goodbye I couldn't help it and that was when I made what I figured was kind of a dumb move.

"Look, Betsy," I said without even thinking about it, "you think maybe it'd be all right to have dinner with me?"

She kinda looked at me, like out of the corners of her eyes, almost like she was worrying about was it a good idea to say yes too soon—anyhow, that was how it seemed to me. So before she could say aye yes or no I told her I knew it must sound funny to her, like maybe I was trying to make a big mad play for her all of a sudden but that wasn't it.

She kept looking at me, only now it was more like she didn't believe a word I was saying and finally I had to laugh—at myself I guess.

"Oh, well," I said, "I guess I might as well level with you, honey. Like I've had nothin' but eyes for you ever since yesterday and here I'm trying to say it ain't nothin' like that. Cause what's the use me tryin' to tell you I'm not makin' a pitch when I really am. So now you know—okay?"

Well, seems like that was about the best thing I could of said cause now she kinda smiled at me and pretty soon she began to laugh.

"You know, Billy? I think I like you," she told me. "At least you're honest, aren't you? You're very sweet, do you know that?"

She's standing right there in front of this big apartment house where she's staying and I'm right there beside her and again it's just like yesterday cause I got all I can do to keep myself from making a grab at her. But naturally I do nothing of the kind, just stand there like the perfect gent, you dig?

"Well, that's nice," I tell her after a couple more seconds. "I'm glad you think so, baby, cause like I sure think you're the livin' end—so how's about what I asked you? You know, dinner?"

She thinks a minute and then she finally says, "All right, Billy."

"Crazy," I said, taking her by the arm and starting to lead her back to my great big blue Caddy sitting out there by the curb.

"Oh, I'll have to change first," she says. "I couldn't go like this."

"Why not?" I said. "My God, honey! You look good enough to eat *instead* o' dinner," I told her. "What do you have to change for?"

She looked up at me and her face got kinda red. I must of been staring at her like I was really getting ready to take a bite out of her—which I guess maybe I damn near was at that.

"No, but I really do have to," she said. Then she kinda laughed and said, "All right, Billy. You've been honest with me so I'll tell you the truth. It's Mother. I think she's out but I have to make sure."

"But like s'posin' she's in and then maybe she won't let you come," I said.

She smiled at me and shook her head.

"I know I can, Billy," she told me. "Don't worry, I'll be out soon. Besides. I really do have to change."

So I hung around outside till she came back out, and then we went and ate ourself a groovey dinner at Chasen's but I had to get her back home before one o'clock on account of the old lady might be coming home then. So nothing much happened that night, except we got to know each other pretty good and by the time I got her home I had bigger eyes than ever.

But after that I didn't see Betsy for about four days. Like I kept on calling her but each time I did she told me she couldn't make it that day. I was beginning to wonder had I done something to make her not like me or something. Only from the way she talked on the phone I could tell it wasn't that, so I figured it must be on account of the old lady, which by this time I'm wishing there was some way I could make her get lost or something.

Then one evening when I was just starting to go out the phone rang and it was Betsy. She had this sexy voice and I started to get all excited from just hearing her on the phone.

"Billy?" she said. "Is that you?"

"It sure ain't Rudy Vallee," I told her. "Hi, baby—what's cookin'?"

"Nothing very thrilling," and she let out that bubbly little laugh of hers. "I was sitting here thinking about you and wondering what you were up to, so I decided to call and find out."

"I'm up to strickly nothin'," I told her. "I was just goin' out to some brokendown restaurant to eat some tired food with a bunch o' stale characters—which I'd a hell of a lot rather be seein' you though. You think like maybe we could arrange somethin', baby?"

I almost flip when she says do I want to come over.

"What?" I said, not believing I was hearing her right. "Over to your place, you mean?"

"That's right," and she laughed again. "Unless you've already made other plans and—"

"The hell with that," I told her. "Don't move, hear? I'll be there before you can say Darryl Zanuck, okay?"

"That's marvelous, Billy, I'm so glad you can come," she said, kinda laughing, and hung up.

I had no idea what the hell it was all about but I got over there in less than fifteen minutes. I rang the doorbell and pretty soon the door opened and it was Betsy and when I got a load of her standing there I goddamn near blew my stack altogether.

Cause all she had on was a negligee like, and it was made out of some kind of stuff you could practically see right through without hardly trying. And by this time I knew her good enough to be pretty sure she wasn't dressed like that because she was too innocent to know what she was doing.

I must have been staring at her like some kind of a jerk cause for a couple of seconds all she did was stand there laughing at me. Then I walked in and closed the door and grabbed her. She was still laughing when I started kissing her but after a few more seconds she stopped laughing and began kissing me back like she meant it.

But all of a sudden she kinda pushed me away and stared at me. I was breathing hard like I'd been running around the block or something and she kept staring into my eyes like she was trying to read some kinda small print written in 'em. I tried to grab her again but she kept holding me off and staring into my eyes like that and after a few more seconds I asked her what goes on.

"I'm trying to see if I can find out something about you, Billy."

"Like f'rinstance?" I said.

"Like . . ." and she kinda bit into her lower lip and I looked down at it and wanted to take a bite myself only she was still holding me off. "Oh," she said, "like whether you're the sort of man who thinks a girl is cheap unless she makes him chase after her for weeks and weeks before letting him see her—" looking down at herself and then back up at me again, "—you know, like this?"

I took a deep breath and then started telling her a whole big thing about how nuts I was about her ever since that first time I got a load of her up at my place and all like that but she put her hand against my mouth and stopped me.

"No, Billy, you don't have to say things like that. I'd rather you didn't, really."

"Why not?" I said. "It's true, baby. I mean it—honest, honey," and I tried to grab her again.

But she pulled away and when I came after her she shook her head and then motioned for me to sit down. So I did and she sat down on a chair a few feet away.

"Okay, so what's it all about, baby?" I asked her. "Why'd you want me to come over here if you won't even le'me tell you how much I want to—how I feel about you or anythin'?"

She sat there for a minute and then she started smiling at me. Only it was a funny kinda smile and all of a sudden she sure didn't look like no seventeen. Like now it was more like *I* was the young kid and she was the grownup woman smiling at some little-kid stunt I'd just pulled.

"What gives, baby? What's goin' on?" I asked her, meantime trying not to keep staring at what was showing through that goddamn negligee thing she had on, only it was awful hard not to no matter how hard I tried. Cause by this time I was like a wild man altogether and I don't know as you can blame me, know what I mean? You should have seen her!

"Look, Billy," she finally said, only now she wasn't smil-

ing. "I just want you to understand one thing before anything else happens between us."

I barely heard what she was saying cause my eyes were
too damn busy for my ears to be working hardly at all. She
stopped talking and made like a little face at me.

"Okay, baby," I told her. "I'm listenin'."

Another couple seconds went by with me just sitting there
staring at her till it's a wonder my eyes didn't jump right
outa my goddamn head and go over there all by themself.

And now she went into a whole long bit about how she
and the old lady had come out here on account of the old
lady thinking she might have a chance of breaking into pictures—Betsy, I mean, not the old lady—only by this time
they both knew nothing was gonna happen so that's why
they were going home pretty soon. She told me about how
her old lady didn't get along so good with her old man who's
a lot older than her old lady and is some kind of a big Wall
Street operator or something and the only reason the old
lady brought Betsy out to Hollywood was she had hopes of
Betsy making the grade and making some kinda career for
herself in pictures so's she—that is the old lady, and by the
way she wasn't that old either cause Betsy told me now she
was only about thirty-seven and still kinda liked to ball a
little bit herself when she latched onto the right guy—but
anyhow what she hoped was for Betsy to make enough loot
in pictures so's she could split out from the old man once
and for all. Cause it seemed she'd just lately started balling
some young bit player she ran into at a cocktail party or
something and Betsy told me a whole lot of stuff about that
and finally she told me this was the first time she'd had a
chance to see me since the first night cause the old lady'd
just gone off to Palm Springs with this young bit player of
hers and so Betsy had the apartment all to herself for the
whole weekend.

"That's why I asked you to come over, Billy," she wound
up. "I didn't know whether we'd have another chance to be

alone together before Mother and I go back home and I did want to see you again before I left."

"Well, that's real nutty," I told her, starting to get up and go over to where she was sitting. "So what are we waitin' for?"

"No, no, just a moment, sweetie." She started laughing at me again. "I still haven't told you what I—"

"My God, baby! I'm about to *flip!*" I told her. "Can't we talk later?" But I sat down again. "Okay, honey, go on. Only . . . whooo-eee!"

She started laughing again but then all of a sudden she got like real serious.

"Look, Billy Miles," she said and it sounded kinda funny for her to say my whole name like that, "I like you. You're terribly sweet and I'm terribly fond of you. I've told you a little about myself and the sort of family I come from and you must know I would have liked to see you before now."

"Sure I do, baby," I said. "But what's all this got to do with—"

"Please, Billy, I'm trying to make you understand something . . . The thing is, I'm not in love with you and I know you're not in love with me either." Except she said eye-ther instead of either.

"But I've been trying to tell you I'm nuts about you, Betsy," I started to tell her. "I've been outa my skull for you ever since—"

"No, Billy, please," she said. "You needn't lie to me. It isn't necessary, honestly it isn't, sweetie. I know exactly how you feel about me. No, please wait and don't interrupt, Billy. You see, I happen to feel exactly the same way about you. It's simply sexual and we've both got a sort of big physical attraction for each other, that's all—and there's nothing wrong with that, is there? But it isn't any reason for us to get things all mixed up and full of lies about love and all that sort of silly nonsense. There's no reason why we can't be perfectly honest about it, both of us, and simply admit what we really feel, is there? I mean, what's wrong with a man and woman wanting to be together when they happen to feel a big phys-ical attraction for each other?"

"Well," I told her, "there ain't a damn thing wrong with it far's I'm concerned, baby. So what's on your mind, Betsy?"

"It isn't anything terribly serious," she said. "At least it needn't be unless you . . ." and she seemed to be kinda think-ing about something. "You see, Billy, I've heard about you. Oh, yes, you have quite a reputation, you know. Don't worry, sweetie—I don't mind a bit. In fact I sort of like it, actually. But the point is you needn't lie about being in love with me or anything of that sort. I think I actually prefer it this way, with the two of us simply being attracted to each other and curious about each other physically, you see, be-cause that makes it fun and keeps things simple and, oh, you know, uncomplicated. Only I do want you to know one thing more about me before we go any further because otherwise it wouldn't be fair to you. You see, Billy, I'm a virgin. Yes, sweetie, honestly I am. I suppose it must sound awfully silly but it's true. . . . And not only that, Billy, but I intend to remain a virgin—until I get married, that is. . . ."

I sure as hell couldn't figure out what I was supposed to say to all this because I sure hadn't been planning on exactly hooking up for keeps with anybody just then. So I just sat there. But I wasn't feeling so hot all of a sudden.

"Don't look so grim, sweetie," she said and now she started smiling again. "It's not as bad as it sounds. I'm only trying to explain something to you. You see, sweetie, I happen to live in a very peculiar and tight little world. I don't suppose I could even make you understand how peculiar it really is. Not that I think you'd care much if I could. Because it isn't a particularly sensible world. Still, it's the one I have to live in. I've never had any choice in the matter, you see. And one of the important rules is that a girl remains a virgin until she's safely married. Do you see, Billy?" and she stopped and waited for me to say something.

"Yeah, I guess I see," I told her.

"Understand, sweetie," she said, smiling at me. "I don't say I like the rule and I certainly would never have agreed to it if anyone had ever bothered to ask me for my opinion of it but—well, there it is. And since I don't think you're especially interested in marrying me at the moment—" she gave out with that little bubbly laugh and looked at me out of the corner of her eyes, "—no, sweetie, please don't be gallant, I couldn't *bear* it if you were. As I was saying, since I realize you aren't going to marry me, and since I'm not at all sure I'd marry you even if you did want me to—well, I didn't want you to have any delusions about what you were getting into, do you see, Billy?"

"Yeah, I guess I see all right, honey." I got up.

Now she jumped up and came over to me and put her hand on my arm.

"Where are you going, Billy?"

"Well," I said, "I don't exactly know, baby, but I figure as long as you're more or less tellin' me—you know, weren't you just kinda tellin' me no soap?"

"Why, of course not, silly," she said. "Nothing of the kind. I was only letting you know what I felt you ought to before we went any further, don't you see?"

"Damn if I do," I said. "You just got through tellin' me you're a virgin and you're gonna keep it that way so I don't dig what I'm supposed to do except cut outa here right now before we start somethin' you don't wanna finish. Or am I bein' dumb or somethin'?"

"No, sweetie," she laughed at me. "Not dumb. But a bit unimaginative certainly, don't you think?"

I still didn't get it and I started to tell her so but just then she reached up and pulled my head down and started kissing me and pretty soon I wasn't interested in talking any more. She had this fine clean smell about her and her mouth tasted almost like wild strawberries, and this time she really kissed me, like she knew what she was doing, and believe me, buddy, she really did know. When we finally broke I was like shaking all over.

"Look, baby," I said, and my voice sounded all hoarse and funny even to me. "I guess I don't really dig all this. What are we supposed to do now?"

She took a step back and opened up the front of that negligee thing so it slipped off her shoulders and—well. . . . There she stood, one short step away smiling up at me and I couldn't hardly stand to even look at her now cause she had the nuttiest body I've ever seen in my whole goddam life, I'm telling you! Man! I was feeling all achey and trembly and I didn't know what the hell I was supposed to do after what she'd just got through telling me.

"Whooo-eee!" I said, breathing so hard I couldn't hardly say another thing. Then I got my voice back. "Listen, baby," I said, "you better tell me to blow right now before I take aholda you and rape you, see?"

All she did was laugh and come right up to me and put herself up against me. And I knew I should split outa here right now, fast, only I couldn't help myself. I grabbed her and held her so tight it was like I was going to bust her right in half and her skin felt like some kinda hot silk under my hands and we stood like that real tight together for a while, maybe not long but it seemed like a million years the way I was feeling right then.

Finally I couldn't make it anymore. I started to push her away so I could open the door and cut out but this time she hung onto me and pressed herself even harder against me.

"Don't go, darling," she was whispering. "Please, Billy, please, please, *please* don't go. Stay here with me, please, darling."

"My *God*, baby!" I said, trying with all my might not to grab her again. "What the hell am I supposed to *do?* I can't take any more o' this!"

She took my hand and started leading me toward another door.

"Come on, Billy, come with me, sweetie," she said as I dragged along after her. "Come *on*, darling," and she looked back at me over her naked shoulder.

"But *what*, baby?" I said. "What's the *use*? You just got through *tellin'* me . . ."

"Never mind, darling," she said. "Don't ask questions," and by this time we're in the bedroom and she closed the door behind me and stood looking at me with a kinda little smile on her kisser.

I shook my head real hard and started to say something else but she stopped me with her hand.

"Don't worry, darling," she told me. "Just hurry up and get your things off and get into bed and—"

"But what the hell, honey," I said, still standing there staring at her body and feeling like the biggest jerk in the world. "Honest, baby, I can't make it this way, like going to bed with you and not do nothin' about it. I'm tellin' you, Betsy, you better le'me cut out o' here before I—"

"Hurry up, sweetie," she said again. "Please, please, hurry up and get your things off. We'll take care of everything in a minute. Only *please*, darling, *hurry!*"

"But what?" I said. As if I didn't have a damn good idea by this time. But there was something about this whole deal that still bothered me, goddamn if I know exactly why.

Still and all that didn't stop me from doing what she said and getting into that sack in a pretty big hurry and after a little while more I wasn't worrying about nothing any more. . . .

So that's how Betsy Huntington and me first got together. And I stayed right there with her for the whole damn weekend and we didn't even bother to go out of the apartment for the two days before her old lady was due to come back.

The real wild part of it all was that here I was, and I'd always figured I knew my way around pretty good by that time, but I'm a liar if this little seventeen-year-old chick didn't show me a few tricks I only heard about before then.

Why, it was like I was the seventeen-year-old and before that weekend was over she'd acted with me like I'm pretty damn sure lots of people don't act with each other even after they been married twenty years.

Only thing I got to say is this:

If that's what these debutante chicks learn by the time they're only seventeen I'd sure as hell be interested in finding out what they're like by the time they grow up and *really* get to know what it's all about.

3

But that was the only time it ever happened. Funny part of it—after that one weekend I wanted no more part of that love nest bit. Not that I didn't still have big eyes for Betsy. Only the way things were I figured enough was enough. Fact I guess maybe I was afraid if we ever got into the hay again I might forget all my good intentions and really rape her, which I'd only kidded her about it that one time. So next time I took Betsy out to dinner I played Papa with her. At first she laughed at me like it was a big gag but pretty soon she got the drift and then she started like pouting and all like that till I finally had to hip her to how I wanted things to be from now on between she and I.

So when she finally saw I really meant it she didn't insist or nothing like that and when I took her home that night she let me kiss her on the cheek and go on home even though she did drop a couple of remarks about the old lady not even coming home at all tonight on account of she was spending most of her nights over at her bit player's pad someplace up in Laurel Canyon. For one second she started to put herself up tight against me again but I took her by the shoulders and held her away and gave her the eye.

"Uh-uh," I told her. "Remember what I told you tonight, baby? Your uncle Billy's cuttin' out right now, got that straight?"

"You're an old sourpuss and I hate you," she told me, kinda flouncing away. But she was laughing a little and I knew she got the idea okay.

Still and all it didn't stop her from keeping on every time I saw her after that. After a couple more times it got to be kinda like a gag with us. Cause there toward the end, she was coming right out and kidding me about it—the whole bit about how she was spending night after night all by herself in that great big double bed and how lonesome she'd get and how a girl liked to be petted once in a while just so's she'd know she had a nice figure and all kinds of crap like that. Kid stuff, you know—but every now and then I'd remember about that one time I'd been with her and then for a second it'd stop being kid stuff, dig?

But anyhow. I'd already made up my mind to play it cool and that's what I did.

Then a few nights before it was time for Betsy and the old lady to leave Hollywood I took her to some party and after it broke up I was feeling kinda restless so I asked her was she sleepy and she told me good God no and we wound up at one of them little after-hour spots they used to have out there on Sunset—you know, out on the Strip?

We had a few snorts just to be doing something but after a while I guess I must of got like a little bored or something. Cause now that the sex department was out I could see Betsy for the young kid she really was, understand? Course she was a kinda well-educated chick, like she read lots of books and all like that—but still and all in plenty of ways she was still pretty wet behind the ears. So about two-thirty, three o'clock, around in there—which by the way that's awful late for Hollywood on account of it's a real square town—I was about ready to go on home and get into the sack and maybe catch up on the sleep bit just for a change.

Then all of a sudden I hear a guy's voice from the front of the joint and it's got kind of a familiar sound. I look up and who do I see but that two-headed no-good bum of a poet buddy of mine. He's standing out there near the entrance with some roly-poly little runt of a guy and the both of 'em are just walking in.

"Hey, Steve!" I hollered.

He looked over and saw me.

"Billy!" he let out a yell. "You old tramp!"

I started toward him and he was coming toward me and we both started hollering and pounding each other on the back and calling each other names and the whole bit and I guess everybody in the joint was staring at us but I didn't give a goddamn I was so glad to see the lanky old bum. Finally we calmed down and then I asked him what the hell he was doing out here and he told me they were making a picture outa one of his things so he figured he might as well come on out and get a load of this Hollywood joint and he just got off the plane about four hours ago and was wondering how to find out where he could get ahold of me and this agent of his told him he'd get him my phone number tomorrow morning but meantime would he like to go and have a fast snort or two so's to settle down after the plane ride and by God if the first guy they run into isn't his old friend Billy Miles and so on and so forth.

Then he interduces me to his agent friend who's been watching us and all of a sudden I remember I've left Betsy all by herself at the table so I turn around but now there's nobody there. Like I'm beginning to wonder what happened to her when I look over and see her down the other end of the joint on her way to the lady's john. For one second I feel a little bad about leaving her like that without even a pardon me. But what the hell, I know I'll square everything soon's she comes back so I tell Steve and his friend to come on over and have a snort at my table, which they say okay.

We're talking up a breeze by the time Betsy comes outa the john. I'm sitting with my back to where she's coming from so I don't even see her till Steve gets on his feet. He's staring at something behind my back and he's got this real wild look in his eyes, like he's seeing something he can't believe is true. So I turn around and here's Betsy coming toward us with a little smile on her kisser. She's looking right at Steve and it's like she's got this deep secret and knows *he* sees she's got it but wants to play games with him and isn't gonna tell him nothing till she's good and ready. Anyhow that's how it looked to me and it all happens right off the bat almost the minute these two get a load of each other and maybe you'll say I'm only imagining it on account of I know now what was gonna happen but believe me, it was nothing like that. Cause this look of hers was something I already knew, dig? Besides I knew Steve damn good by this time and in all the years I knew him I never seen him look at any broad like he's now looking at Betsy. So I know goddamn well I'm not just making all this up, see?

I got the drift almost that first second and in the few more seconds it takes me to interduce everybody all around and all like that, I already know just what I'm gonna do. First I make sure Betsy sits right across the table from Steve so's they can keep on digging each other if they feel like it. Which they do all right, except by the time they kinda get ahold of themself again they don't do it quite so open. But I can see 'em sneaking looks at each other when they think nobody's noticing so I know everything's cool and they're gonna make it okay.

About ten, fifteen minutes later I make an excuse to get up from the table, like I'm going to the can. Soon's I'm behind Betsy's chair so she can't see me I look over at Steve and give him the eye. Then I head for the can and pretty soon here he comes. He's still looking kinda glassy-eyed but I don't say anything about Betsy at first—you know, I'm waiting for him to bring it up, on account of I'm getting a real bang outa seeing old Steve all worked up over this chick.

But he didn't crack. All he did was look at me like he wanted to know what gives. So I waited.

"What's up, Billy?" he finally asks me. "What did you signal me about?"

"Nothin'," I said, real deadpan. "Like I just wanted to talk to you is all. What the hell, man, I ain't seen you in over five, six months now. What's new?"

"Oh," he said. He had that kind of a dignified look a guy sometimes gets when he knows he's being ribbed but don't wanna let on he knows, know the kinda look I mean?

I had to bust out laughing at him.

"What's the matter?" he asked me.

"You dig her, huh?" I said, grinning at him.

Instead of answering me he started getting red all over his face and neck. I had to laugh even harder. My God! Steve Larsen blushing—I'm telling you, man, it was too much! I thought I'd split a gut.

"Dig who?" he said, like he didn't even know what I was talking about. "Who do you mean, Billy?"

"Hey—come-*mahn!* Steve! This is Billy—your boy Billy, 'member me? I'm with *you,* pal. I could see how you were starin' at Betsy—it's okay, you don't hafta hide nothin' from your boy."

"Oh! Miss Huntington, you mean!" he said, like he'd just that second got hip. "Why, yes—I think she's wonderful, if that's what you mean."

"Ah, come on, Steve," I said, still laughing at how he was trying to act like it didn't mean a damn thing to him one way or the other. "Look, le'me straighten you out. She's nothin' but a friend o' mine, see? So quit actin' like that. It's okay by me. Fact I'm tickled to death. You want her? Okay, go make it—how's that?"

He got a look on his homely kisser like a kid seeing his first Christmas tree.

"Seriously, Billy? You mean it? You really don't care about her?" He just couldn't believe a guy could look at Betsy and not care about her.

I said sure I meant it. Not only that, I told him, but I'd even make like some kind of an excuse to cut out and leave her with him so's he could get a little better acquainted with her himself.

"But how do you know how she'll feel about that?" he asked me. Now he was worried again.

"Don't worry, Steve. Like I got a pretty good idea she won't mind." I had to laugh again at how he looked at me when I told him that.

"Why?" he said. "She couldn't have told you anything, Billy." He sounded like a nine-year-old kid. "I was there all the time so how could she have—"

"Listen, you character," I told him. "You're a big man with the word department but when it comes to chicks you don't know which end is up—you know that, don't you?"

I grinned at him and he grinned back but his face got red again. He wanted to believe me but like he still couldn't believe it was okay.

"Look," I told him. "She had big eyes for you from the first second she saw you. What's the matter with you, don't you think I know? I been watchin' you two ever since she came back to the table. Don't worry about it, Steve—if you like her, quit worryin'. Everything's gonna be real crazy, just take my word."

"But what are you going to do, Billy?" he asked me. "I mean to say, I wouldn't want you to make it too obvious. I don't want her to think we'd gotten together and talked the whole thing over. You know." He was real serious and he kept on looking at me with that worried look.

"Listen, leave this to Uncle Billy," I told him. "You stick to writin' and le'me handle this department. Only le'me give you one little tip, Steve. She's only a young kid, understand? I got an idea she's prob'ly still a virgin. Course I don't know, you understand. But I got an idea she is. So like don't get too worked up about it, see?"

He was staring at me like I'd said something real awful, almost like I'd just insulted him or something.

"For God's sake, Billy," he said, "what kind of a heel do you think I am?"

I had to laugh at him.

"I didn't mean it like that, Steve," I told him. "All I'm

doin', like I'm tellin' you the score, is all. You got the ball
from here on in so I just want you to know what it's all
about, see what I mean?"

He gave me a kinda suspicious look.

"How do you know so much about her, Billy?" he asked
me. "Didn't you say you were only friends?"

For one second I was gonna hip him. But I saw the look
on his face and I figured the hell with it, why drag him. And
besides, strictly speaking, Betsy and me didn't *really* make
it—what I mean, she really *was* a virgin, all right, far's *I*
knew anyhow, so why should I put her down before he even
got a chance to find out if he really dug her, know what I
mean? And anyhow she was leaving town in a few more days
so the hell with it. Let the guy get his kicks. You know what
I mean—how'd I know how things were gonna work out?
What I mean—well, I guess all I'm trying to say is, when
you came right down to it what the hell business was it of
mine, right?

So I didn't tell him.

"I just kinda got like a hunch about her," I said. "That's all
it is, Steve. Come on, let's go."

We went back to the table and pretty soon we decided to
cut out, the whole four of us. Steve's agent grabbed the
check and Steve started arguing with him how he was gonna
pay it himself and I figured while they were straightening
that out I'd get a chance to talk to Betsy alone. So I told
Steve to settle it any way he wanted to and I'd get even with
him later on and meantime Betsy'n me'd be waiting outside.

"Well, baby," I said when we got out on the sidewalk,
"looks like Steve's got big eyes for you. Guess you musta
noticed it yourself, didn't you?"

"Has he?" she said, like it didn't mean a thing to her if he
did or he didn't.

"You know damn well he has," I said, laughing at her.
"Come on, don't gi'me that baby-face bit—I know you real
good by now. You didn't miss nothin' back there, I was
diggin' you all the while."

All of a sudden she gave out with that bubbly little laugh and handed me that look outa the corner of her eyes.

"You're really terribly cute, Billy," she said.

"Yeah," I told her. "Like you're pretty damn cute yourself. And not only that but I know good and goddamn well you're hip. Right?"

She laughed again.

"Well?" I asked her. "So how's about it?"

"What do you mean, Billy? How's about what, sweetie?"

"You'n Steve, you know what," I told her. "And you better hurry up and le'me know before he comes out here. Like he's a real bashful guy so I don't think it'd be a good idea to let him know we're talkin' it up like this, understand, honey?"

"He *is* Stephen A. Larsen, isn't he?" she said with a kinda faraway look in her eyes. "I mean, *the* Stephen A. Larsen, isn't he, Billy?"

"Yeah, I guess so," I told her. "Anyhow I don't know any other ones. But what's that got to do with it? What I wanna know is do you want me to get lost and let him take you home tonight or don't you?"

"Well . . ." she said. "Did you ask him?"

"Sure I did. What do you say?"

"What did he say?" she wanted to know.

"I'm tellin' you, the guy's got big eyes," I told her.

"Isn't that strange," she said, and it was like she was talking to herself. "Isn't it sort of strange and wonderful? All the times I've read his books and wondered what sort of a man he really was and now I meet him and you tell me he likes me and. . . ."

"Hey! Here they come!" I butted in. "What do you say, Betsy? Hurry up before they get here."

"Of course," she said, talking real low as they came over to us. "Certainly, Billy—and Billy?"

"Yeah?" I said. They were almost over to us now.

"Thank you, sweetie," she whispered in my ear. "Thank you very much—for everything."

I looked at her. Her eyes were all kinda shiny and now

Steve and the other guy came up to us and she turned them shiny eyes of hers on Steve and I could see from the way he looked at her and then real quick over at me that he had the whole deal all straight.

It wasn't too tough for me to find an excuse to cut out and leave the both of 'em together. Steve's agent friend said he was pretty pooped himself and if nobody minded he thought he'd be running along home.

Steve and Betsy just sat there looking at each other, like they'd both just made some kinda big discovery. Man! I've heard a lot about this love-at-first-sight bit but this was the first time I ever did see it right up close like that. Must be real crazy when it happens to you. Me, I'm still waiting. . . .

4

So that's how Steve'n Betsy come to know each other in the first place. Which in a way I guess I feel kinda like responsible for everything that happened, on account of if it hadn't of been for me bringing 'em together they probably never would of even met each other and things couldn't of turned out like they finally did. Course on the other hand, how're you supposed to know what's gonna happen with a guy and a chick. And besides I figured when Betsy and her old lady left town that'd be the end of it.

Some end. Hell, that was just the beginning. This whole thing between 'em was like one of them big prairie fires where everything is all nice and quiet and peaceful till all of a sudden somebody lets a spark fly and next thing you know all hell is popping all over the place and looks like the whole damn world is blazing like mad.

Next day Steve came over to my place and for the rest of the afternoon all I heard from him was Betsy this and Betsy that and Betsy the other thing till it was coming outa my ears. Talk about having it bad! Man! He *really* had it.

He gave me the whole treatment—how wonderful she was and how this was the one chick in the whole wide world he's been looking for all his life and so on and so forth. I remember one time he called her something like a not impossible she—or anyhow it sounded something like that and I didn't wanna stop him and ask him what the hell that meant on account of he was all wound up and going real good and I always did like to hear Steve go when he was going good.

Finally he ran outa gas and I asked him how long he was gonna stick around town. I told him Hollywood was kinda square and all like that but still and all we'd have some laughs cause I knew a few real kookey types I wanted to have him meet.

He looked at me like I was flipping or something.

"Hollywood?" he said. "Who needs it? Who wants it?"

"Ah, it ain't that bad," I told him. "We'll have a few yaks, you'll see." I started telling him about some of them real squares working in The Industry, like they always called the picture racket out there, and then I started talking about some of the stuff we could do around town. You think he even heard me? I might as well of been talking to the wall. He let me go on for a while and then he busted in and started telling me all about Betsy again, like I never even met the chick for God's sake.

"Okay, Steve," I said when he finally come up for another breath of air, "I guess I got the general idea. So all right. Long's you're that hung up on her go ahead'n see her for the rest o' the time she's out here. But soon's she's gone we can start makin' a few plans for—"

"As soon as she's gone I'm gone with her," he said. "What's the matter with you? Think I'm going to let her go back East so someone else can have a chance at her? Not me, fella, not by the longest shot you ever played. This is the girl I've been waiting for all my life and I'm not fool enough to let her get away now that I've finally caught up with her."

I stared at the guy. He was serious.

"Mean to tell me you're cuttin' out just when you got here?"

"You're damned right I am."

"Well," I said. "I don't know what the hell to say to that." I was kinda brought down, you know?

"There isn't anything to say, Billy," he said, grinning at me. "Of course you might try wishing me luck."

"Okay, so I wish you luck," I told him. "Hell, you sound like you're thinkin' o' gettin' married or somethin'."

"That's precisely what I am thinking of, Billy," he said, absolutely deadpan.

This time I *really* couldn't think of one single thing to say. Not that I had anything against Betsy, cause what the hell, she was okay. But after I had already spent that one week-end with her, it made me feel kinda funny to hear my buddy telling me he was gonna marry a little chick who'd—well, I mean *you* know. But naturally I couldn't tell him about that—specially now that I knew he was real serious about her. So all I said was had he told Betsy about him going back with her.

He told me sure he had and Betsy was tickled pink.

"I see," I told him. "Well—crazy, Steve."

"You sure sound enthusiastic," he said, grinning at me. Then he got serious and gave me a kinda funny look. "What's the matter, Billy, don't you like Betsy?"

"Me?" I said. "Why shouldn't I like her? What do you mean? Think I'd of interduced you to her if I had anythin' against her? It's only that I was kinda hopin' you'd stick around a while so's we could have a few laughs and all like that, that's all." What the hell could I tell him?

So that was that. I didn't hardly even see him again and a few days later he was on his way back East on the same train as Betsy and her old lady. He called me up before he got on the train but the rest of the time before leaving he was with Betsy practically every minute of the day and for all I know maybe the night too. Cause I do know that the last few nights in Hollywood Betsy's old lady stayed with her bit player all the time and knowing Betsy like I did I figured maybe she was giving old Steve that same workout she gave me that one time. Course I can't swear to that, naturally, cause Steve's not the type guy to talk about a thing like that, not even to his best pal. But after they left town I got to thinking and then I remembered that time she told me about how she was damn well gonna stay a virgin till she got married and all like that and then I got to figuring that if she really gave old Steve the same bit I got that one weekend— well, it wasn't too hard for me to understand how a guy like him could get so hooked on her he'd be ready to do just about anything, including get married to her.

Now right here I gotta make one thing clear before I go ahead with all this. I just been reading over the last part of what I been putting down here and I guess maybe it might look like I think Betsy tricked Steve into marrying her with the old sexaroo department. But that's not exactly what I meant to say. Like I told Steve, Betsy was okay with me. I can't put her down, what the hell, cause she leveled with me right off the bat, see? And you can't blame a chick for making up her mind to stay a virgin for her husband, even though you don't run into too many chicks like that nowadays. What I mean, that's no rap against her. Maybe what I'm trying to say is this—and it's really two things:

One is that it had to be *me* of all guys who'd been through that weekend with her. And the other thing, I just couldn't see these two together—I mean married. You know—she was a nice enough chick and all that but she was awful young and wet-behind-the-ears. Besides, and maybe *I'm* being all wet here, but it seemed to me like they come outa altogether different worlds, dig? Cause Betsy really was one of them society type chicks all right, the genuwine article, like they say. And Steve—well, I already told you about the kind of character he was and the world he come outa. Not that he was a bum by no means. Steve had plenty of class in his own way even if he didn't know from clothes and fancy table manners and that bit. What the hell, he'd spent most of his life hanging around with them bums and dips and hoods and junkies around them joints in Chicago. Hell, that was the big reason why he was able to write the kinda stuff he did—which by the way, just going by what Betsy'd told me about having read his stuff, it must of meant that even them real high-society palookas liked his stuff just as much as us lowbrows did, if you know what I'm getting at. But all I'm saying, I couldn't see 'em together, that's all, cause I couldn't figure how two characters coming outa such different worlds, like they did, could ever get married to each other and make sense out of it.

Now, I don't want you to think I'm saying all this just to prove what a smart citizen I am or nothing like that. Cause I realize I might of been way off the beam in how I figured it, and I've seen plenty of weird marriages with all kinds of knocked-out characters and lots of 'em make it okay, I guess —or anyhow they look like they do. So for all I know maybe Steve and Betsy could of made it at that. It sure as hell looked like they were doing all right there for quite awhile.

5

I'm gonna like skim over the next few years—cause all I knew was what I'd hear from Steve when I'd run into him every once in a while. Or else from somebody who knew the both of us and would give me a fast rundown on 'em now and then.

I saw Steve and Betsy together a few times when I'd come to town. Like I'd run into 'em at the Stork or some trap like that. By that time it was already a great big thing with the both of 'em. I never did see two characters so stuck on each other.

This went on like for a year, year and a half, and then next thing I heard they finally got married. I was out on the coast when that happened so I couldn't come to the wedding. And about a year later they had a kid and then about a year and a half later they had another kid, both of 'em little girls, and then after that they had still another kid—only the last one was a boy.

Meantime Steve is batting out book after book and each one of 'em's even madder'n the one before and it looks like he's really hit the jackpot on account of all you're hearing all over the joint is Stephen A. Larsen this and that and the other thing. Seems like everybody in the whole damn United States including Texas is reading his stuff. He's got pieces in all the different magazines and somebody writes a smash play outa one of his things and that's also made into a movie, which this one's a hit too and with all that, the cabbage is rolling in like Steve bought up a piece of the U. S. Mint or something.

So things keep on like that for about three more years and then the war comes and Steve is drafted just like everybody else and pretty soon he's shipped out to the South Pacific and I don't see nothing of him for a long time on account of I'm over in Europe doing a hitch in the brown gown myself. So finally after the war's all over I'm back in my own racket again where I belong, working a four-week engagement at the Chez in Chicago and packing 'em in, if you'll excuse me for saying it except it's the God's honest truth so help me.

Anyhow . . .

I finish the last show one night and I'm up in my dressing room changing my clothes. I'm kinda beat and feeling a little brought down and all like that. All of a sudden there's a rap on my dressing room door and when Zoots, that's my dresser, goes to open the door who is standing out there but Steve and Betsy! Well, I'm telling you, man, the next minute it's like Old Home Week and the whole three of us are jabbering and hollering at each other and laughing up a storm and nobody's listening to nobody and everything is real nutty again.

So pretty soon we cut out of there and go someplace and

have a ball telling each other what's been happening, and I never been so glad to see anybody in my life as I was to see these two characters. Betsy looked fine. Course, she wasn't the young chick she used to be when I first knew her but still and all, on her it looked crazy. Steve looked kinda beat up to me but after all he always did look a little beat up anyhow. Only I don't know—I kinda got the idea he wasn't feeling so hot. He had like a look about him, specially in his eyes. But he was just as mad as always and he kept on saying these wild things like he always was able to think up and the whole three of us were juicing it up pretty good and laughing and cutting up old touches, so pretty soon I figured it must of been only my imagination on account of I haven't seen the guy in such a long time and kinda forgot how he looked, know what I mean?

At least that was what I figured till the next day when I got up around two o'clock, real hung over, and waited for him and Betsy to call me up like he'd said they would. We were gonna go over to the Pump Room and have maybe like a couple Bloody Marys apiece and then hang around and eat dinner together and after that they were coming over to the Chez and catch my show and wait till I finished up so's we could go out and have another ball—or something like that anyhow. So I get up and have like about a gallon of coffee while I'm sitting around waiting for 'em to call or show up or something.

So I wait and I wait and nothing happens, nobody shows. They never did show. Or even call up. Nothing. Not that day or the next day or any other day. And I can't figure out what the hell happened till about a week later I get a note from Steve. Here's all it said:

Dear Billy,

You are one of our favorite people. Betsy and I are back in New York and I'm hard at work again. Please look us up when you come to town. We are living at—(and he wrote down the

address, likewise the phone number)—so give us a blast when you
get back. Good luck, old friend.

As ever,
Steve

That's all it said. Like not even an explanation why he
never called or showed up like he said he was gonna—nothing but this note.

But still and all I didn't give it a lot of thought even
though it did seem kinda funny that all of a sudden he decided he hadda get back to work just like that, out of a clear
blue sky, you might say. A few months later when I'm back
in New York I give 'em a call and they seem real knocked
out to hear from me and we see each other a few times and I
bring over some toys for the kids and the whole bit and it's
real happy times all over the place, see?

But meantime I begin to notice something kinda funny,
almost like Steve is two different guys. Like one time he'll be
tickled to death to see me and just like it's always been with
us. But like every once in a while he'll kinda clam up and
start acting weird and then I can't find him at all. I don't
know if I can exactly explain what I mean but like there's
something working on his mind and he's changed in some
weird way. And when he's this way it's kinda uncomfortable
being around him. I mean, it's a real drag, on account of he
acts almost like there's something about me he don't like.
Which naturally I try to ignore it on account of it makes no
sense till all of a sudden after all these years it dawns on me
about maybe Betsy's gone and told him all about she and I
that one time back there in Hollywood. But still and all that
don't make much sense either. Cause if she did tell him, why
should he act one way with me one time and then another
way at other times?

So now I can't figure it out at all and after a while it starts
dragging me. Cause no doubt about it, Steve *is* acting kinda
funny.

Like take the time I run into Mack Glover—you know, the

columnist? I'm sitting in the Cub Room with some broad having a couple snorts and Mack spots me and comes over to talk it up a while. Just before he leaves the table he says something almost throws me for a loop.

"Well, Billy, I guess I'll see you tomorrow night," he says.

"Tomorrow night?"

"At Steve's birthday party," he says, giving me a look. Mack's a pretty sharp little guy.

"Oh sure—course," I told him. "Guess I must be gettin' absent-minded in my old age."

Naturally I don't want Mack to know I don't even know Steve's having a party so then I say something about I got another date but I'm gonna try to make it anyhow. Besides I still don't know—maybe Steve only forgot to let me know about it and I'll still get a call from him, you know? I figure I'll wait like till tomorrow and by that time I'm sure to hear from him cause I never heard of Steve pitching any kind of a ball without I'm asked to be there—that is if I'm in town, which he sure as hell knows I am on account of we saw each other only three, four nights back.

But by now the whole thing is prying on my mind like, know what I mean? Like no matter how hard I keep telling myself to forget it, maybe he just forgot to call me or something—still and all I *can't* forget it. So then I figure the hell with it, let me call up my hotel and find out right now so's I can get the goddamn thing offa my mind, see?

Nothing doing. I ask 'em at the desk have they got any messages for me. There's a couple calls but nothing from Steve. By this time I'm feeling a little hot. So I ask for the operator and tell her I been expecting a call from a Mr. Stephen Larsen and did she by any chance forget to mark it down and leave it in my box. You know, I wanna be good and sure.

She says no, there's been no calls for me except the ones in my box, and what's the matter with me, did I think she didn't know how to do her job, and so on and so forth, real salty, yatata, yatata, till I finally hadda hang up on her right in the middle of a sentence—which I guess I didn't miss nothing at that.

Now I'm starting to burn. Sure, I know it's silly but all I'm telling you is what happened, not how much sense I was making, dig?

By this time it's about two o'clock and by the time I get back to my chick I got it figured out how to find out if Steve didn't call me just by accident or if it really meant he didn't *want* me to come to his goddamn party. I just wanted to know, that's all. I mean you know—either we're buddies or we're not. A guy likes to know these things, right?

So next day about three, four o'clock in the afternoon I call Steve. He comes on the phone and sounds just like he always does. You know—"Hi there, Billy old friend," and the whole bit. So I toss the crap right back at him and meantime I'm waiting to see will he make a crack about why don't I drop by tonight on account of he's having this party.

Think he even mentioned it?

So then I wanna make sure it ain't maybe some kinda surprise and he prob'ly doesn't even know he's having a party, so I talk to Betsy. But she don't make any cracks either. So finally I talk to Steve again and ask how about him and Betsy meeting me later on and we'll go out someplace and have a couple snorts and all like that—just to see what he'll say to that.

"Gee, I'd love to, Billy," he says, real smooth, "but I can't tonight. I've got a slight touch of grippe or some stupid thing like that and I think if I just stay in tonight and get to bed early I may be able to knock the damn thing out before it gets worse. . . ." And blah-blah-blah and then he started talking about why don't we make it some other night soon—you know, first chance I get and all that kinda crud—so now I figure I know how things stand.

After we say goodbye and hang up I got the thing pegged one of two ways. Either Betsy's finally told him that story about the time we were together—or else, and this'll show you how hard it was for me to believe what was really going on, maybe Mack Glover's made some kinda mistake about them having a party at all. Cause I still can't believe Steve or Betsy'd be lying to me about something like that, not after all this time.

When I finish up my last show that night the damn thing's beginning to really work on me. Finally it got me down so bad I knew I hadda do something and then's when I got the idea how I could find out for sure, one way or the other—the hell with it, just so I knew for sure.

I go into a phone booth and call Steve's number and when he comes on the phone I got a pencil stuck between my teeth and I talk real high and ask can I please talk to Mack Glover. Sure enough Mack's there all right and while I'm waiting for him to come on the phone I hear a whole bunch of people talking and laughing and carrying on, so now I know and as soon as Mack comes on I hang up cause I sure as hell don't wanna talk to *him* about nothing.

I spend the rest of that night getting real fractured. Later on I run into a few cats I know and we go from one joint to another one, lushing it up pretty good and yakking about nothing at all. And all the time, inside I'm cursing that god-damn little bitch of a Betsy Larsen. By the time I fall into my pad about six o'clock in the morning I got her pegged for the prize bitch of all time for having ruined the whole long palship that'd gone on between Steve and I just cause I once had a fast little scene with her.

But I was all wrong. I might as well tell you that right here even though I didn't find it out till quite a while later on, not till after her and Steve got divorced and I saw her one time later on and asked her right out if she told him. And just in case you think maybe I was being a sucker to believe her I might as well tell you part of why I know she wasn't lying to me.

Cause after the divorce Steve started coming around again

just like nothing ever happened. Which I know damn well he wouldn't of if Betsy'd ever of told him about she and I having once spent a whole weekend in bed together—or anyhow damn near a whole weekend even though I guess we did get up once in a while during those couple days— you know, to eat and stuff like that.

Course by the time I did see Steve again it wouldn't of mattered much to me if I never saw him again, on account of by then I'd made up my mind the hell with it if that's how he wanted it to be. But then when we got back together again, I don't know—pretty soon we were buddies again. What the hell, why not? Like I said before, the guy was lots of laughs and after all we'd been pals all these years, so what's the difference if he did act kinda weird for a while there just before he and Betsy got divorced. I figured it might even of been on account of whatever it was that was going on between 'em that finally led to them splitting up and maybe that was the reason why he'd acted so funny during that time, know what I mean?

Anyhow that's what I thought. I didn't know what the divorce was all about and it was none of my business cause how're you gonna ask a guy about something like that? I mean you know. He'd mention Betsy once in a while when he got a little juiced but he never would say much except how he missed the kids and all like that and I sure as hell wasn't gonna ask him why they got divorced in the first place. Besides he probably wouldn't of told me even if I did ask. I know Steve and he never was the kinda guy to go around crying on nobody's shoulder. Except the one time he did it with me—but that was later on.

6

All of a sudden one day Steve disappeared. I started asking around but it looked like nobody had any idea where the hell the guy'd gone to. It was almost like he just went away and fell right offa the edge of the earth. It wasn't till about six, seven months after he cut out like that that I even had the slightest idea where he went to.

I was out the coast on another one of them picture deals and one night I was at some party and run into that same little roly-poly guy'd been with Steve that night I interduced him and Betsy. We got to talking about Steve and he ups and tells me he's just got a letter from him.

"You did?" I ask him. "Well, where the hell is he for God's sake?"

"India," the guy tells me.

"What's he doin' in India?" I ask him.

"He's in Calcutta," he says, like that explains the whole thing.

"Look, I'm kind of a dope," I tell him. "So maybe that's why I don't dig what this Calcutta's got to do with anything. I mean, like what the hell's he doin' in India?"

He kinda laughs and then he tells me he can't understand it any better'n I do and the letter sure as hell don't make things any clearer. All it says, it says Steve's in training for the annual marathon swim down the Ganges River or some such name as that. Course I know Steve can't swim a stroke so naturally that's just one of them silly gags a guy writes when he's got nothing to say except hello or something like that.

"Is that all?" I ask the guy. "I mean, like isn't there anythin' about how long he's gonna stay there or when he's comin' back or nothin'?"

"No, that was about all he wrote," the guy tells me. "He said he was training hard because he feels it would be a great honor for an American writer to win the marathon. Oh, yes—he also mentioned that the toughest competitor he would have to beat is the entry from Egypt who is an excellent swimmer, a three-year-old crocodile by the name of Archie Fitzjoggins who developed a new variation on the

Australian Crawl while he was a don at Oxford." He looks at me and starts laughing. "That Steve," he says, shaking his head.

"Yeah," I tell him, "he's really somethin'," and we both laugh and that's that.

Well, one night after I get back to New York I'm out in some trap with a few cats and all of a sudden I look over and see a guy and a chick at a table across the dance floor and who do you think it is? It's Betsy Larsen, which I haven't seen her in a hell of a long time, not since even before the divorce.

At first I'm not even gonna talk to her. But she looks up and spots me and waves for me to come over so naturally I can't ignore her. So I start over there to give her a fast hello. Only when I get near the table I almost turn around and go back cause now I see who she's sitting with and he's a wrongo from away back, a playboy type jerk who's always around with some showgirl or model lushing it up on account of this is the only way he can figure out to help his family get rid of all the cabbage they got stashed away in just about every bank in the whole wide world including maybe even Calcutta, India. His name is Howie Randall the Third. So help me, that's it—and the gag around town is, whenever anybody mentions his name they call him the third-and-I-hope-the-last, or else Howie Randall the Turd, so maybe that'll give you some idea.

Anyhow, Betsy interduces me to this jerk—which I already been interduced to him like maybe twenty or ninety times but each time I make out like I don't remember him and naturally that makes him most happy to see me on account of by this time he's hip I'm only doing it to put him on. So after I say glad to meet you and he says again how we've already met and then I answer oh have we, like I can't remember him, I finally sit down. By the time I leave I can tell they got a whole big thing going on, these two, and when I get back to my own table again I look over a couple times and they're staring in each other's eyes like they both just discovered they could see for the first time, know what I mean?

Funny thing though, all the time I'm with 'em Betsy don't mention Steve. So I don't say nothing either. I figure why stick my nose in? What the hell, is it my business if she wants to make a goddamn fool outa herself?

A few weeks later on I'm working this four-week engagement at the Paramount, and one afternoon I'm out on the stage doing the bit and when I look down there is Betsy sitting there in the second row staring up at me like she's one of them bobby soxers or something. I damn near break up altogether and I can see she knows I spotted her cause she gives me one of them little smiles of hers like a cat that's just caught itself a canary and is trying to figure out does it wanna start in on which wing first.

After I get off she comes backstage—and this is the time I mentioned before, when I finally asked her if she'd ever told Steve about she and I.

Well, she swears up and down how she'd never even breathed a word of it to Steve on account of how jealous he always was of her—and all I can tell you, I gotta believe her the way she tells me this on account of I'm watching her real close when I ask her about it and nobody in the world can lie that good. Anyhow, after that she tells me she's just heard about Steve being on his way back to New York.

"You've got to help me, Billy," she says. "He wrote and said he wants to talk to me about a reconciliation and he'll be back within the next few weeks."

"Help you?" I ask her. "What am *I* supposed to do for God's sake? What do you wanna do, baby—you wanna go back with him?"

"How can I?" she says. "How can I go back to Steve when I'm in love with Howie Randall," and she must really like this jerk all right cause she even leaves out that the-Third gimmick—not to mention the and-I-hope-the-last.

But I can't see myself butting into this scene and I start

telling her that, but then she busts out crying and talking about how I'm an old friend of the family and all like that and if I won't help her who's she gonna turn to and so on and so forth and pretty soon I can't help it on account of I can't stand that crying scene. So I ask her what does she want me to do and okay already, stop crying and I'll try and do it, whatever the hell it is. Now she stops crying and looks up at me and her eyes are all wet and shiny and all of a sudden I remember how she looked at Steve that time outside that joint on the Strip and I start thinking what a goddamn shame it is they ever split up.

"Listen, Betsy," I tell her. "You sure you don't wanna go back with Steve again? I mean, can't you get over it—you know, whatever you busted up about?"

She looks at me like she's about to say something, but then she stops and shakes her head and says no, no, no, no, no, she can't possibly ever go back to him again, not after what happened and all like that only she never does crack about what did happen.

"Well, then," I tell her, "why don't you just tell Steve what you're tellin' me and maybe that'll end the whole hassle. I mean, what can I do any more'n that?"

"But you can talk to him, Billy," she says. "You know him well enough to talk to him. Tell him I don't want to go back to him. Tell him I'm in love with someone else. Anything—you'll know what to say, Billy. I can't—I never could talk to him. Maybe he'll listen to you."

"But my God, honey!" I said. "How can I butt in and tell a guy a thing like that? What the hell, you're the one has to tell him. Besides he'n me ain't exactly like we used to be, you know? Fact that's why I wondered if you maybe told him about us that one time out the coast—cause he kinda changed. I guess we're still friends and all like that, but it's different."

"Yes, I imagine it is," she said. "But it has nothing to do with you and me, Billy." She stopped and gave me a kinda funny look and then she said, "You see, there *is* something I never told you—only I can't tell you now or you'll refuse to help me. And you've got to do this for me. Please, Billy, please do it for me!"

Well, she kept on begging and pleading with me till finally I had to tell her okay, I'd try to tell him—that is if I saw him when he got back, which by this time I was starting to hope maybe I wouldn't on account of I didn't wanna get tangled up with something like this where, after all, what can I wind up with except maybe a great big headache, know what I mean?

Still and all I feel kinda sorry for Betsy—specially after what she told me about being in love with this no-goodnik of a Randall-the-Third type. So after she leaves I get to thinking about it and the windup is I start figuring maybe I do owe her at least this much. Cause, after all, I'd been the one brought 'em together in the first place so maybe it was up to me to try and get her to maybe make another stab at it with Steve. I mean you know, I still figured it was one of those things oughta be patched up on account of Steve being worth a hundred and thirty-eight Howie Randall the Thirds in my books any old time—whether we were still pals any more or not.

Which that goes to show how wrong you can be.

Anyhow, about three, four weeks later I got a call from Steve.

He told me he just got back to town and he wanted to see me right away, it was awful important. So I told him come on by and pick me up backstage right after the last show.

7

Well. . . . You never seen a guy so changed in your life. If it hadn't of been I knew him so long I'd of hardly even recognized him when he walked in the door. He was even skinnier'n he used to be—which I've already told you he always was pretty goddamn skinny to begin with. His hair looked like nobody'd put a comb to it all the time he's been away and he needed a shave real bad and on top of that his clothes hung on him like somebody put a big sack over a skeleton or something. Like I said, Steve always did dress like a tramp comic anyhow, but now he looked like something'd been standing out in the rain for about a month. And with it all he had this kinda different look on his kisser—like a sad, miserable look. Fact he looked to me like a guy's about to bust out bawling or something.

At first he tried to act like the same old Steve—you know, making mad cracks and carrying on just like he always used to, but by the time we left and got over to my place and had a couple bourbons he began to slow down and pretty soon he came to a dead stop.

Course I'd already asked him what the hell he'd been doing all this time way the hell and gone out in this India joint for the love of God. All he told me was he was learning about that yoga or some bit like that so I figured he was ribbing me and I let it go at that. But now I asked him again.

This time he looked at me for a long time before he started talking.

"All right, Billy," he said. "I'll try to explain but I'm warning you, it may sound very strange. I don't want you to think I'm crazy but some of what I'm about to say may sound pretty strange to you."

I had to laugh, he was so damn serious.

"Okay, Steve," I said. "Only since when did *you* start worryin' about soundin' crazy?"

But he didn't even smile so I shut my yap and listened.

All I can say is this was some of the wildest stuff I ever did hear—even from Steve. Course I've heard people talk about yoga this and yoga that. Remember when Lou Nova was going around shooting his big mouth off about how he was gonna take Joe Louis with that cosmic punch of his that he got from some Yogi character down there in Jersey some-place? But I always figured it for some kinda gag for old ladies or else for screwballs who didn't know no better, see? Now here was Steve Larsen giving me a whole long spiel about how he's been spending the last ten months doing some kinda mad exercises with some type of a swami charac-ter out there in this India and how he's already—and this is exactly like he said it, so help me—achieved the first four stages and how all this yoga bit has changed his whole life around so he's seeing things altogether different now.

One time when he was in the middle of telling me some-thing about one of these stages and some of the weird exer-cises he had to learn to do before he could attain that stage—which that's how *he* said it—he all of a sudden sat down on the floor and got himself all doubled up like some kinda contortionist with them long skinny legs of his all curled up and his big feet way up around his ears. And then after he got himself all wound up like that he looked up at me with them sad-looking eyes of his and I just couldn't help it, I bust out laughing and I couldn't stop. And the more he looked at me and the sadder his eyes got the more I hadda laugh at him, till toward the end there I figured I was gonna bust if I couldn't stop.

Finally I quit laughing and meantime Steve's untangling himself. Now he gets up and sits down on his chair again and looks at me.

"I'm sorry, Steve," I told him. "Only you looked so god-damn comical sittin' there on the floor all twisted up like some kinda pretzel, know what I mean?" and I bust out laughing again.

All he did, he sat there looking at me till I got all finished and he didn't get sore or nothing like that, just waited till I got all through laughing.

"Well, Billy," he said, after I kinda calmed down, "I told you you'd think it was strange."

"Whooo-eee!" I said. "Man, that ain't strange! That's real

knocked out—how'd you ever learn to do somethin' like that?"

"Well anyway," he said, still looking real serious at me, "perhaps that'll give you a sort of general idea."

"Yeah, it sure as hell does," I told him, kinda grinning. "So now I know what you been doin' all this time. Studyin' up on how to be a contortionist, right?"

He didn't answer me right away. Course I was pretty damn sure it wasn't all this malarkey about learning how to be a contortionist. Still and all, I'm kinda getting my kicks outa this whole new *mishugas* of Steve's. Only thing, no matter what I say he won't laugh. And after a while more I begin to get hip he's really changed—not only just the way he looks either, you know?

Finally I get it through my noggin this ain't the same Steve Larsen I used to know. I don't know what it is about him or why all this yoga jazz should of made such a big difference in him but one thing is for sure. He is different all right and not only that but if you ask me this is no improvement over the old Steve but just the opposite. Still and all I'm kinda curious to hear what he wants to talk to me about. Also I still remember my promise to Betsy so I wait for him to tell me what he's got on his mind.

Pretty soon he starts talking and sure enough it turns out to be about Betsy. And it's just about the biggest tale of woe I ever did hear. Fact it gets so bad that pretty soon I'm like starting to get a little embarrassed. He tells me all about how he feels about the kids and how much he misses 'em and the whole bit, and it's like he's just now discovered about families—cause that's all he talks about, how a family's gotta stick together, how nobody's got a right to bust up a family, and so on and so forth, and I'm just starting to wonder where does Betsy come into all this when he starts in on her. He tells me how nuts he is about her and how lonesome he is and how he's gotta get her back and how he almost killed himself when they got divorced, except he finally figured he'd cut out and try and pull himself together and that's how come he went to this Calcutta joint but now he's gotta get Betsy and the kids back and like straighten out his life again. And he goes on and on and *on* like that for a hell of a while and I'm telling you, man, in a way it's enough to make a guy bust out laughing except in another way it's so goddamn sad and miserable-sounding you can't hardly keep from crying the way he tells it. Specially Steve, cause like I said, he's never been a guy for talking too much about personal stuff like this even though he can talk forever when it comes to just talking, you understand.

"So you see, Billy," he finally winds up, "that's why I had to see you, old friend. I want you to help me."

"Me?" I ask him. "How?"

Like I don't already know.

"I want you to talk to Betsy," he says. "I know she thinks of you as one of our dearest friends, Billy. She's always thought a lot of you and—well, I thought you might be able to persuade her to let me have a serious talk with her. Will you do it, Billy?"

"Gosh, I don't know, Steve," I tell him.

I'm like trying to stall. I mean, like I'm trying to figure how to get outa telling him what Betsy made me promise I would—you know, I don't wanna be the one to break it to him about this Howie Randall the Turd and all like that, know what I mean?

Turns out he already knows about it though.

"Of course," he says, "I suppose she's spending most of her time with this Randall kid but—oh, sure, Billy, I heard about that before I left India. You know, you can get United States newspapers in Calcutta too and it's been in all the columns, I suppose you must have seen something about it yourself, haven't you?"

"Yeah, I read somethin' about it," I told him.

"I can't believe she's really serious about this," he said after a few seconds. "I called her and begged her to let me

talk to her but she refused. She said I could come up any
time and visit the children but she refuses to see me herself."

"Well," I said. "Like maybe she really likes this Randall
character."

"I can't believe it," he told me, shaking his head and looking over at me. "I mean to say, "I've heard about this Randall
boy and I can't believe a girl like Betsy would ever take a
kid like that seriously, can you, Billy?"

"Gosh, I don't know, Steve," I told him. "I mean you
know. Like after all you know Betsy better'n I do."

"That's just why I can't believe she's serious about this,"
he said. And he stopped, like he was waiting for me to agree
with him.

"Well, maybe you're right, Steve," I told him.

"I know I am," he said. Only there was something about
the way he said it made me think maybe he wasn't so sure at
that.

I didn't say nothing.

"Well, Billy, old friend?" he finally said. "What do you
say? Will you talk to Betsy? Will you try to get her to let me
see her, just once?"

He looked so pathetic and miserable I couldn't help myself. I still didn't really wanna get into all this, even after my
promise to Betsy, but now I hadda tell him okay, I'd try and
see what I could do.

"That's wonderful, Billy," he said and this was the first
time he even smiled all night. "I knew I could count on you,
old friend."

"Ah, what the hell, Steve," I told him.

8

Next day I called Betsy and told her I gotta talk to
her. She asked me what happened but I told her I'll give her
the whole scoop when I see her. At first she sounds almost

like she don't even wanna talk about it but finally she says okay.

So that night after the last show I go over to her apartment. This is the first time I've been there since before Steve'n her got divorced and it seems kinda funny without Steve there. I mean, Steve was always making a big racket around the house but now it's kinda quiet and like empty, almost like somebody's died or something.

Well, we sat down and I told her what Steve'd told me about how he felt about her and the kids and all like that and then I told her how he wanted to talk to her about wasn't there some chance of them getting back together again, and all the rest of it just like Steve told me last night.

When I got all finished she said, "Do you believe Steve's still in love with me, Billy?"

"Course he is," I told her. "Listen, honey, I know Steve real good and I know he'd of never told me the stuff he did without he was still stuck on you. Like he practically got down on his knees and begged me to talk to you so's he could come up here and tell you himself. And you know Steve's the last guy in the world to beg anybody to do him a favor. What the hell, Betsy—I don't have to tell you."

She gave me a funny look.

"No, you don't have to tell me, Billy," she said.

"All right, all right, so what goes?" I asked her. "You wanna be stubborn? What's the use?"

"I told you, Billy. I'm in love with Howie Randall."

I felt like telling her what a jerk this guy is but I stopped myself.

"Okay, so you're in love with him," I told her. "So what harm can it do to *see* Steve'n tell him yourself. Course if you want me to butt out, okay, Betsy—but still and all I can't see how it's gonna hurt you to just see the guy and—"

"Look, Billy, it's not that it would hurt me. Only . . ." and she didn't finish what she was gonna say.

"Only what?"

She kinda thought a minute and then it was like she'd just made up her mind about something.

"Billy," she said. "Did Steve ever mention anything about why we were divorced? I mean, did he tell you the reason for it?"

"No, he didn't say nothin' about that. Why? What's that got to do with it?"

"It's the only thing that *has* anything to do with it," she told me. "You see, Billy, there was one big reason why our marriage blew up. Actually it was the reason I never should have married him in the first place. I suppose I'm as much to blame as anyone else—if not more so. Of course—" and she kinda gave a little laugh, "—I know he couldn't have told you the reason we were divorced. He wouldn't have dared, I knew that before I even asked you."

By now I'm wondering what the hell is this all about. But she sits there not saying a word and finally I ask her what goes on and will she please let me know what she's driving at.

"All right, Billy," she says, with that same funny laugh, "I'll let you in on the deep dark secret. And you'd better hold onto your hat, because I think you're going to be pretty shocked."

"Oh, fine," I said. "Listen, baby, I know Steve a long time and if there's anythin' you can tell me about that guy can shock me—well, this I gotta hear."

"Don't laugh, Billy," she said, real serious. "Just you listen and then see what you think."

"Okay, I'm listenin'," I said, still kinda grinning. But in about three seconds flat I stopped grinning.

"Well, in the first place," she starts off, "you know I'm half Jewish, don't you, Billy?"

"You're—*you're* half *Jewish?*" I busted out.

She smiled and shook her head up and down a couple times.

I just sat there staring at her. I couldn't believe it. Betsy looks about as Jewish as—as I don't know what, and here I'd known her all this time and never even—but then I stopped and thought for a second and I realized most people don't know I'm Jewish either so what am I being so surprised at? You see, my real name ain't Billy Miles at all, that's only like a stage name I took when I first started in singing and figured my own name was no good for show business, know what I mean? Joseph Malovitz, that's my real monicker, see? Maybe you can see how it'd be damn tough for a guy name of Joe Malovitz to get very far with them bobby soxers, not that I'm trying to say they're against Jews or nothing like that cause I'm not a guy goes around getting into those kinda arguments. I always figure the hell with it, I'll let people who dig these things do the arguing. Maybe you'll say I'm wrong but look—who wants to go around looking for trouble, know what I mean? You know, I never denied it but still and all I don't see what's there to go around shooting my mouth off about it either, right? I'm doing okay so why go looking for headaches? And don't think I feel bad about it, cause I don't, see?

The hell with it, let me go on about Betsy.

"Yes, Mother is Jewish," she was saying. "And I suppose she probably feels pretty much the same as you do about it, Billy. Considers it a sort of unfortunate fact and tries to ignore it. Oh, stop looking at me like that, of course I know about your being Jewish, silly. I've known it from the first time I met you. I've never thought about it one way or the other. I'm sure you'll agree that I'm scarcely what anyone might call a professional Jew. Besides, since I'm only Jewish on Mother's side and *she* certainly doesn't go around bragging about it I always thought I could be either a Gentile or a Jew, just as I chose. The fact is I've never had any real occasion to think about it much, either way. Oh, of course I've heard remarks now and then, at school or when I was with people who didn't know about me—but I've never encountered enough of it for it to become a *thing* with me, as it does with lots of people. Besides, I don't happen to look much like what people think of as Jewish so I suppose it just doesn't occur to them. As a matter of fact I suppose most of my friends don't even know it. I've never talked much about it and somehow—I can't exactly explain it—but it just doesn't seem to come up and since I don't go out of my way to bring it up—well, there you are."

"Well, are you—I mean, well, you know—" I said, not knowing just how to say this but I was kinda curious so I went ahead and said it anyhow. "What I mean, Betsy, were you ever—oh, you know, ashamed of it?"

She didn't say nothing right away, just seemed to be thinking about it.

"Frankly," she said finally, "I don't know how to answer that question, Billy. It may be that I sort of retreated from the idea of it when I was a little girl and perhaps there was a certain amount of shame connected with it. But I can't tell you truthfully because I honestly don't know. Of course I knew Mother was Jewish but since she didn't mention it I may have got the idea that it was something one didn't speak about. What it all adds up to, is that I'm not religious at all, that is not in any organized, church way, and on the whole I've never seen where it makes much difference one way or another. Do you, Billy?"

"Gosh, I don't know, honey," I told her. "I guess I never did think about it very much. You know me, baby, I just mind my own business and try'n have a ball best way I can."

"Yes," and she laughed a little. "Perhaps that's actually the only sensible thing to do."

"So—you were sayin' about you'n Steve," I finally said.

"Oh, yes, of course," she said. "Well . . . You remember when I met him, Billy. You know what a baby I was. Well, there was Steve, the great Stephen A. Larsen, the famous writer right in the middle of his glamorous career—everything I'd ever dreamt of in a man. The moment I saw him and knew who he was I fell head over heels in love. But you know, I've often wondered, Billy—perhaps it was never really Steve I fell in love with, maybe it was only someone I thought he was—you know, having read his things and all. Anyway, when you told me that he liked me too—well, it was simply too wonderful to be true. And finally when Steve said he loved me and was coming back to New York just because I was, I couldn't bear it. I think that was about the happiest I've ever been in my life."

She got up now and started walking up and down while she kept on talking.

"After we came back to New York," she said, "we saw each other as often as we could. At first Daddy was against the idea of my becoming involved with Steve. He always called people like that bohemians—still does. Daddy's terribly stuffy and strait-laced and all that sort of nonsense and I suppose he had some other sort of man in mind for me—probably some nice square young stockbroker or something of that sort. Mother, of course, is—oh, well, you know Mother," and she looked at me and laughed.

"Oh, sure, I remember mama," I said. "Boy, they sure sound like a weird combo, them two. How do you suppose a pair like that ever got together in the first place, huh, Betsy?"

"That's quite a story all by itself," she said. She gave out another one of those little laughs but it was easy enough to see she didn't think it was so funny. "But anyway," she said, "to get back—I was so mad about Steve I couldn't think of anyone else and after a while Daddy began to see there was nothing much he was going to be able to do about it. For a while he threatened to send me off to Europe with Mother but I refused to go and I told him I'd run away from home if he tried to force me. I was so in love I couldn't see straight. And the wonderful part of it was that Steve seemed to be in love with me too. Honestly, Billy, I used to wonder sometimes if I wasn't dreaming the whole thing—and even right now, looking back at it, it still seems pretty crazy, the way it all happened."

"Listen," I said, "I was there, remember me? I saw how it was."

"Yes, but there was one thing you didn't see, Billy," she told me. "And the ridiculous thing is that I was childish enough to think it couldn't really matter. My God! How giddy can you be? But honestly, I truly believed it was only a small thing and couldn't possibly make any difference in the way Steve and I felt about each other."

"What are you talkin' about, Betsy?" I asked her. "Come on, tell me."

She gave me a kinda funny look outa the corners of her eyes.

"Very well," she said. "You see, Billy, one night when Steve and I were having dinner with a couple of his friends he suddenly launched into one of the most vicious anti-Semitic tirades I've ever heard in my life."

I was looking at her like she'd gone outa her mind.

"*Steve?*" I busted out. "What the hell are you talkin' about, Betsy? Steve couldn't of done nothin' like that! How can you even say a thing like that? What's the matter, don't you think I know the guy?"

"It's true, Billy," she said and the way she said it I let her go on talking. "Believe me, it happened, just as I've told you. Actually it was worse than I can possibly tell you. I suppose I must have flinched a little, or something, because he turned on me and said—in a nasty voice, not at all the way he ordinarily talks, you know—anyway, 'What's the matter with *you?*' he said. 'What are *you* looking at me like that for? *You're* not a Jew.' And right then and there, Billy, was when the whole stinking mess began. Because you see, I behaved almost automatically—out of fear of losing him, or causing a scene, or Lord knows what. It might have been nothing more than extreme embarrassment for him, shame at the spectacle he was making of himself, or even just plain stu-

pidity on my part. In any case, I know I couldn't possibly
have behaved differently under the circumstances and it's no
use to pretend I could have, not the way I'd been brought up
and the kind of a girl I was. I just shook my head and sort of
shrank inside myself and said, 'Why, no, Steve, of *course* I'm
not.' And naturally that fixed it once and for all. From then
on, you see, I was trapped. And as time went on and somehow Steve never found out about it, it kept getting worse
and worse until I finally began to realize that the only way I
could ever get out of this awful trap I'd caught myself in was
to make a clean start with him, even if it meant ending the
whole thing between us—because after a while it got worse
instead of better."

I just stared at her.

"The point is, though," she said, "I simply couldn't bring
myself to tell him. I kept putting it off and the longer that
went on, of course, the harder it became to get myself to
think of telling him and losing him—as I was sure I would.
Oh, I know. I know how awful all this makes me sound. The
truth is I'm so ashamed of myself I wasn't going to tell you
about it even tonight. But I'm so sick and tired of the whole
idiotic, rotten mess that I may as well tell you and then
you'll see how impossible the whole thing is and always has
been right from the very beginning."

I must of been staring at her kinda funny cause she came
over and sat down and asked me what was I thinking about.

I shook my head.

She laughed a little.

"Yes, I know," she said. "And I'll bet I know just what's
going through your mind. 'Not Steve!' That's what you're
thinking. 'Not Steve, of all people—Steve Larsen, the man
who loves people, the great compassionate lover of mankind.
Steve Larsen an anti-Semite? Impossible! Why, look at all
his Jewish friends in the theatre, in motion-pictures, every-
where—it can't be true!' Isn't that what you were thinking?"

"Well, I don't know," I told her. "Maybe it was somethin'
like that. Except I was wonderin' about somethin' else too? I

mean, like Steve knows *I'm* Jewish. I mean, I never tried to
hide it from him."

"Look, Billy," she said with a little smile on her face, "I
once told you, a long time ago, you're very naïve. At times
I've wondered whether you weren't pretending to be a lot
more naïve than you actually are, but after all these years
I'm beginning to believe you really are that way."

"Thanks a lot," I told her, "but what's that got to do with
anythin'? What's my bein' naïve got to do with Steve knowin'
I'm Jewish?"

"You're inclined to overlook one thing, Billy—you happen
to be a big name."

"So?"

"Steve happens to like people with big names," she said.
She shrugged her shoulders. "It's as simple as that. He likes
two kinds of people. Characters—those are good to write
about. And big names—because those are good to be seen
with."

"But for God's sake, Betsy! Steve's a big name himself.
What the hell's he need *my* name for?"

"He doesn't, silly—not any more than he needs Mack
Glover for instance. You know Mack is Jewish, don't you?"

"Yeah, sure I know, but—"

"But Mack also happens to write a rather important col-
umn, don't you see? Look, Billy, stop fooling yourself about
Steve. He's a whole lot shrewder than you realize. Just stop
and think for a moment. Can you think of one single person
he's ever been really close to who hasn't in some way been
good for him? Or who isn't a celebrity of some sort? Think
about it, Billy."

I did. And you know something? She was dead right. By
this time I was starting to feel real evil. But still and all, at
the same time I still couldn't make myself believe it's really
true, know what I mean?

"Okay, baby," I said. "So go ahead. Like I might as well
hear the whole thing, long as we come this far."

"Very well," she said. "Anyway, finally Steve asked me to

marry him. He wanted us to get married immediately but I
kept telling myself over and over, 'No—I've simply got to
tell him about myself, no matter what happens—I've got to
or else I can't marry him'—but I still didn't tell him. And the
insane part of it is that I was more in love with him by then
than ever. That is if you can call a thing like that love. At
any rate, I didn't tell him and in the end we got married—
and I still hadn't told him."

She stopped and looked at me.

"It makes a lovely picture, doesn't it, Billy?"

"Yeah, sure," I said, shaking my head.

She shrugged her shoulders.

"Well," she said, "all this time the same kind of thing had
been going on. Every so often Steve would burst into one of
those tirades of his. 'Those dirty, scummy, slimey, filthy Jew
sons-of-bitches,' he used to call them. 'The clever people'—
that was another pet phrase of his. He used to say it over
and over till I thought I'd go out of my *mind*. Oh, yes—'Defilers of the earth,' that was one of his more poetic phrases. I
remember once when he'd made a deal with a Jewish producer who was putting on a play that had been made out of
one of Steve's things. Jay Rossen did the dramatization—you
know Jay, don't you? Well, it doesn't matter. Every time
Steve came home from seeing this poor man he would start
in on those 'dirty, no-good, miserable, slimey kike bastards,
those filthy defilers of the earth—oh, those scummy clever
people'—I tell you, Billy, there were times when it got so—
so psychopathic it made my hair stand on end."

I took a breath and let it out and then I lit up a couple
cigarettes and handed her one.

"Still," Betsy said, "somehow we kept going along. We had
our first baby, Susan, and then Linda, and then little Howie
—funny, isn't it, that I should now be in love with Howie
Randall—you really ought to know him, Billy, he's a wonderful boy when you get to know him."

I didn't say nothing. Why the hell should I? By this time I

couldn't see how she could do a hell of a lot worse'n she's already done with the guy *I'd* interduced her to.

"But all through those years when I was having the children," she was saying, "I used to have absolute nightmares whenever I'd think about this—this cancer that was growing between Steve and me. Finally I realized that our marriage would come to a complete dead end if I didn't do something to save it. I was desperate. I knew I had to tell Steve but the more I thought about it the more impossible it was for me to face it. And all that time this anti-Semitic thing of his became even worse, if that's possible. Because there's nothing rational about it in Steve's case—that is if you can ever call anything like that rational to begin with. I mean, with Steve it's even more irrational than with other people I've known who have the same attitude toward Jews. You see, Billy, his mother has it too. Perhaps he got it from her in the first place. I remember when I'd spend a little time with her whenever we visited Chicago, take her shopping with me, as I did from time to time to please Steve, because you know how fond of her he is. Sometimes when we'd start to go into some shop she would take me by the arm and lead me away and whisper in my ear like some old witch. 'Nah, nah, Betsy,' she'd croak, 'nah, not in there. Those are Jews who run that store. Stay away from the Jews'—and she'd drag it out between her teeth so it sounded like some sort of a terrible curse. 'The Jew-w-w-ws,' she'd say, 'they're gree-ee-eedy. Gree-ee-eedy people, no good, dirty people. Stay away from Jew-w-w-ws,' and she'd carry on like that until I began to feel all slimy and dirty myself! Why, that old bag! Talk about being greedy! And dirty! That horrible old bitch could give anyone cards and spades when it comes to being a mess! You've met her, haven't you, Billy?"

I said yeah I'd met her but I didn't say nothing else. What was the use of saying anything about some old lady probably don't know no better anyhow, know what I mean?

"Well, anyway," Betsy went on, "after Steve left for the

war I had lots of time to think. And I finally decided that
when he came home I'd have to tell him the whole thing.
Because by that time we'd been married long enough, and
now with the children and all—I couldn't see that it could
make much difference any longer. Well, after he got back we
moved into this apartment and things began to settle down.
But I still couldn't figure out how to break it to him. Because
after he was discharged from the Navy he was even worse
than before the war. Why, one time when I tried to say
something to him while he was in one of those tantrums he'd
get into about the Jews, he turned on me like a wild animal
and snarled at me to shut up, told me I didn't know what I
was talking about. I got so angry that I almost told him then.
Instead, though, I said he was beginning to sound like Hitler. All he did was laugh and say, 'Don't kid yourself, little
girl. Hitler wasn't so wrong and there are plenty of people
around who are finally beginning to realize that.' I was so
mad I was about to tell him to take a good look at his wife
then—but I was afraid of him, the way he looked at me, and
I couldn't get myself to say it. Not for another couple of
years."

"Whoo-eee!" I said. "Like you two cats must of really had
yourself one hell of a married life outa all this!"

"You know, Billy," she said, dead serious, "—actually it
wasn't as bad as it sounds. Oh, I know how that must sound
to you—but it truly wasn't. Because you see, this sort of
thing didn't go on all the time. It was only now and then,
and at other times Steve was wonderful. You know how
much fun he can be when he's feeling good and most of the
time he was altogeth—"

"Yeah, sure," I told her. "Some fun."

"Oh, well," she said. "Never mind, what's the difference
now?"

"Plenty of difference," I told her. "I'm sorry, Betsy, but I
guess maybe there must be somethin' the matter with me
cause I'll be goddamned if I can see any fun about any of
this you been tellin' me."

"I suppose you're right," she said. "Anyway—I kept waiting for the right time to break it to Steve and finally it
seemed to me the right time had come. We were getting
along wonderfully. Steve had just finished another book and
his last one was doing fine and for once he seemed to be
feeling good about everything. It had been weeks since he'd
even made the slightest remark about Jews or anything of
that sort and I believe things between us were better than
they'd ever been. He was beginning to talk about having
another child and this was the first time he'd mentioned
anything like that since getting out of the Navy, you see. So
one evening when we were home having a drink and listening to some music I decided I might just as well break the
whole thing wide open and tell him what I'd been trying to
tell him all these years. I handled it quite cleverly, I think. I
mean, I was very careful not to break it to him too bluntly
because I wanted to be clever about it. Clever . . . 'Clever
people'—maybe he was right when he called us that, do you
think, Billy?"

She gave me a smile so's I could see she didn't mean it the
way it sounded. I waited for her to go on.

"In any case," she finally said, "I must say, I broke it quite
gently. I started out by asking him if he loved me. 'Of course
I do,' he said. I remember he was reading the paper. I went
over and sat in his lap. 'No, Steve,' I said. 'I mean, do you
really love me? A lot, I mean.'

" 'More than anything in the world,' he said.

" 'And the children?' I asked him. 'You do love them, don't
you, Steve?'

" 'Of course I do, sweetheart,' he said. 'Why, you and the
kids are my whole life, you know that. You're everything on
earth to me.'

" 'And nothing on earth can change that, can it, Steve?' I
asked him. 'I mean, nothing will ever stop that, will it?'

" 'Nothing in the world, sweetheart,' he said.

"Then I got up and looked at him and said, 'All right,
Steve'—and there must have been something about the way

my voice sounded because I was scared to death and sort of out of breath. He suddenly looked up and said, 'What's the matter, Betsy?' I told him I had something I had to say to him and now he was staring at me in the strangest way but I forced myself to go on with it.

"'I've been wanting to tell you this for a long, long time, Steve,' I said. 'Only I've never been able to get myself to do it before. But now I've got to if we're going to go on together.'

"He put his drink down and looked at me and said, 'Well, tell me. Is it something that's happened since we were married? Tell me!'

"'No, Steve,' I said, and I almost started to giggle. 'No, it's nothing that happened since we were married. It happened long before I ever met you. It's something that happened long before I was even born.' And then I told him. I just looked him right in the eye and said, 'You see, Steve—I'm half Jewish.'

"Well, Billy—you'd have had to be there to believe it. It was incredible."

She stopped talking and kinda shook her head and a look came in her eyes like she was just now seeing the whole thing happening again.

"What happened?" I asked her. "What'd he say?"

"He just stared at me," she told me after a few more seconds. "But the *way* he stared. The way his eyes looked. His whole face seemed to fall apart. It was as if I'd put a match to him and was watching him melt and run apart like a wax candle. It was just too horrible! And then he got hold of himself. And began saying things. Like only Steve can. Only this was like nothing I'd ever heard in my entire life before, from him or anyone else. He sounded like an absolute maniac. He cursed and screamed and spat at me as if I were some filthy, loathsome—well, not a human being but an *object.* As if I were a *toad,* all covered with warts. Or slime. I've never had anyone look at me like that in my life. I can't

remember very much about what I did. All I do know is that
in the end he left. Got up and walked out. That's all. But I
can tell you one thing. If I live to be a thousand years old I'll
never forget the look on his face when I told him. There's no
way to describe it."

After she got through, we both sat there for about a minute. Finally I turned and looked over at her. "And that was
it?"

"Actually, no," she said. "Oddly enough, he came back
several days later and told me he'd decided we had to talk
the whole thing over. We had to figure things out—that was
what he said." She let out a laugh and looked down at the
floor.

"What did you tell him?" I asked her.

"Oh, I went along with it." She shrugged her shoulders.
"By that time it didn't matter. As far as I was concerned
nothing Steve could ever say or do would ever make a great
deal of difference to me any more. Or at least that's what I
thought."

"But what'd he want?" I asked her. "I mean, what the hell
was there to figure out?"

She told me they had this long talk. They went on talking
for a couple days and meantime Steve came back to the
apartment. But they didn't stay together. He slept in one
bedroom and Betsy slept in another one. The idea was, Steve
kept saying, they had to figure out if there was some way for
'em to keep on living together.

"For the kiddies, naturally," Betsy told me. She gave a
nasty little laugh. "You've heard him about the kiddies,
haven't you? Nothing must ever hurt the kiddies, I always
say. Steve always used to say it too. Till it came out of my
ears. Oh, I don't know—I suppose I'm being bitter—" and
she kinda laughed again. "Perhaps he honestly meant it. I'll
bet that's the line he used to get you up here tonight,
wasn't it?"

I told her yeah, maybe it was at that come to think about

it. I was starting to feel kinda real dumb, know what I mean? Also a little sick at my stomach too.

"Of course," she said. "Good old Steve. Why, do you know what I did one evening while we were still—figuring things out?"

She looked at me and laughed.

"Steve had been carrying on about what I'd done to him. Finally I couldn't stand it any longer. I was wearing a nightgown and I walked over in front of him and then I ripped it down the front and stood there about two feet away from him screaming at him like some old fishwife. 'Here, take a good look!' I screamed. 'See? See how slimey and dirty and filthy and scummy I am? See what an ugly old toad you married? Look at the warts all over my body, take a good look at the evil Jew bitch who bore your children! Why, you ugly, miserable, horrible, evil-minded creature! I'm as white and clean as anyone you've ever seen in your whole life! You! With all that yellow hair all over you! You should talk about people being ugly and filthy and slimey! Why, you don't even bathe regularly—you smell bad!'"

All of a sudden she stopped and began to giggle like she was hysterical or something. But then she got ahold of herself and looked at me and laughed.

"Because you know, Billy? Steve really didn't bathe very regularly. I was always after him to keep himself clean and have his hair cut and things like that."

"Yeah," I said. "I guess Steve never did care a hell of a lot about that kinda stuff."

"Even that isn't quite true," she told me. "He had enough vanity. Except in his case it seemed to work in reverse, you see."

"Well," I said. "So what finally happened?"

"Well," she said, "a few nights later we decided to try to get our minds off ourselves for a little while. Go to a movie or something. We went over to the Sutton Theatre and after the movie we came out and began walking toward Lexington Avenue. And that was when the strangest thing happened. I don't know if I can make you understand this exactly, but as we walked along I kept seeing these people walking toward us on the sidewalk coming the other way. Women. It seemed as if there were nothing but women on the street that night. Women carrying bundles, women with children, women in mink coats, shabby women, old women, young women, women of all sorts and sizes and different ages. But the craziest thing—they were all . . . Well, it seemed as if they were all caricatures. Remember the sort of thing Goebbels used to circulate in the Nazi papers during the war? Those hideous, exaggerated, distorted things? I kept telling myself it wasn't real, that this was only what Steve was seeing. 'It can't be true,' I tried to tell myself. 'It's only because of the way he's been talking to me. My God! What's the matter with me? I mustn't let myself get all neurotic and crazy because of all this. It's not true, it isn't even true that Steve's seeing them this way. I'm only imagining things. Maybe I'm going mad, maybe these aren't even real people. I've got to stop it before I do go mad!' This went on the whole length of the block between Third and Lexington. And then I suddenly learned it was true, that Steve had been seeing them the way I had imagined he was, or I had been seeing them the way he imagined them—I'm all mixed up but you see what I'm trying to say, don't you, Billy?"

"Yeah, I see, but what made you know it was true?" I asked her.

"Steve," she said. "All at once he turned on me and began cursing and screaming like a madman right there on the sidewalk with people passing and staring at us—but he didn't even see them, he couldn't seem to see anything. He was absolutely insane. He tore off his hat, flung it down on the sidewalk, and jumped on it with both feet. 'Did you see those goddamn filthy kikes?' he snarled at me. 'Did you get a good look at those ugly, slimey, scummy Jew bitches?' By that time it didn't even sound like Steve any more, because he was all hoarse and his voice would crack and now and then it broke altogether and went way up high, almost to a scream. 'Jesus God!' he screamed. *You're* not like that! You're a beautiful white rose, not one of those ugly, miserable kike bitches! You!'—and his eyes had a mad glare in them, 'How can anything like you grow out of that dirty, filthy, scummy slime? Sweet Jesus Christ! What you've done to me! You've made my kids into dirty kikes like yourself and your rotten, filthy kind! I've got to get away from here because if I stand here and look at you any longer I'll *kill* you for what you've done to me, you stinking, slimey, slut of a filthy Jew bitch!' Oh dear God! The things he called me."

Now she stopped and everything got real quiet. I didn't look at her—I was feeling kinda crawly.

"Well, Billy," she finally said. "There you are . . ."

I let out a big sigh but I didn't say nothing and I still couldn't get myself to look at her.

"That was the last, bitter end," she was saying. "He walked off down the street and left me standing there."

"You never saw him again?" I asked her.

"Oh," she said, kinda shrugging a little, like what the hell difference did it make, "he called up the next day to find out when it would be convenient for him to come and get his things—you know, books, records, papers, personal things of that sort. I arranged to be out when he came to get them. And that was the end. That is aside from the formality of the divorce."

"Goddamn!" I busted out now. "You realize what you been tellin' me, Betsy? You sure you're not like exaggerating any o' this. Like it's awful hard to believe a guy like Steve could of ever—"

"No, Billy," she said. "Believe me, I'm not exaggerating anything. Do you think I could make all this up out of thin air?"

"No, not that, only—well, like it's pretty tough to take without wonderin' if maybe—"

"Listen, I'll tell you one more thing," she said. "I mentioned Jay Rossen a while ago, remember? The man who did one of the dramatizations of Steve's things?"

"Yeah," I said. "What about him?"

"Jay and Ella Rossen were good friends of ours. When Jay heard about our split-up he came to see me. Of course he knew nothing of what I've just told you. He simply thought he might be of some help. I tried to tell him there was nothing he could do, that Steve and I were going to be divorced, but he wanted to go see Steve and have a talk with him. I knew he was hoping to patch things up between us somehow. I was frantic at the idea of his even going to see Steve. I told him I didn't want anything at all, just a divorce, I didn't care about anything else and please not to go. Because you see, Billy, Jay is Jewish. Well, I did everything I could to stop him but he wouldn't listen. In the end I had to tell him the whole story. Jay is the only other person in the world outside of Mother and Daddy, and now you, that I've ever told any of this to."

"Well, what did Jay do after you told him?" I asked her.

"He was like you," she said. "He wouldn't believe it either."

"Well, there you are," I said. "What the hell, you can't blame the guy, I mean, this is a rough rap to hang on anybody, specially a guy like Steve, you know."

"But it's the truth," she told me. "Rossen knows it now."

"How's he know?" I asked her. "Steve didn't tell him anythin', did he? What happened?"

"Well, when Jay talked to Steve that first time—he went to see him in spite of anything I could say—he told me afterwards that he thought he detected certain—oh, you know, sparks, during their conversation. But because he was determined not to accept what I'd told him, he forced himself to overlook everything, thinking it was what I'd said that was acting as a sort of poison, making him feel things that weren't really so, you see."

"Why, did Steve make any cracks?" I asked her.

"Oh, of course not," she said. "The way Jay finally learned I hadn't lied to him was quite accidental. Several weeks later he was having lunch with some people, in connection with some play that was being produced. As it happened, none of the other men at the table were Jewish. There was Lewis Andrews—you know, the producer? And Cecil Williamson, the director. People like that, all theatre people, you see. Anyway, sometime during lunch Steve's name happened to come up and at that point Andrews, who has known Jay for a long time, said, 'That rotten bastard! How does a nice guy like you get mixed up with a rotten son-of-a-bitch like Larsen, will you tell me that, Jay?' Which made Jay indignant. He turned to Andrews and said, 'Why? What have you got against Larsen? That first show of his you put on did all right for you, didn't it?' And Andrews said, 'Look, Jay, maybe I shouldn't be telling you this but I work with lots of Jewish people in my business and I'm not going to hand you any of that hooey about some of my best friends being Jews, but you do happen to be an old friend of mine and I don't understand what the hell you see in a bastard like Larsen. He's one of the most sickening anti-Semites I've ever encountered in my life. I wouldn't want a fellow like that around me for five minutes, hit play or no hit play. I never have been able to understand how you can stand him. I know I couldn't, and I'm not even Jewish.' There was more along the same line, Jay told me the next time he saw me— but that was enough, of course, and that was what finally convinced him. If you still don't believe me, I'd suggest you give Jay Rossen a call and ask him."

I looked at her and shook my head.

"Whooo-eee!" was about all I could say.

"Yes, Billy," she said, shaking her head up and down and smiling at me kinda sad like. "Whooo-eee is right."

I got outa there a little while after that. What the hell was there left to talk about? Besides I was feeling kinda slimey and scummy and filthy myself. My pal Steve Larsen! Like all I wanted was to get home and try'n forget I'd ever even heard of Steve Larsen.

9

So—there's that part of it. Course I'll never really know the whole thing on account of how's anybody ever gonna know all the real ins and outs of a thing like this? All I'm saying, I don't know how much Betsy might of left out about what part she really had in it. Cause what the hell, let's face it, I know damn well there's gotta be more to it than she'd of told me—maybe even more'n she knows her own self, dig?

But anyhow I finally figured out a gimmick so's I could find out for sure about the part of it was really bugging me. What I did, I called Betsy up and told her I want to write down what she told me and show it to Steve and would she mind if I did that? She said not at all, for me to go right ahead and show it to him. With her compliments. So that's what I did. I didn't say nothing to Steve about any of this till I got all finished writing the whole thing down, all about how Betsy'n him come to bust up. Meantime I stalled Steve, told him I called Betsy up and was gonna see her in a few days and all like that.

Then when I got it all written down in black and white I called him up and asked him to come on over to my joint. He showed up and started calling me old friend and the whole bit, just like always. I didn't make a crack, just handed him what I'd written down and told him I'd like to have him read it over and see did he think it was any good, you know, him being a pro and me being nothing but a real amateur at this writing racket.

He looked at me kinda surprised.

"Why, sure, Billy," he says, and I can see he figures I'm pulling some kinda gag on him or something. "But when did you start writing? I had no idea you were ever interested in trying to write."

"Ah, you know," I told him. "Once in a while I sit down and fool around. Like for kicks, that's all it is. Read it over, will you, Steve? See what you think about it."

So he sits down and starts reading. And by the time he's read the first few lines I can see his face kinda change. But he don't say nothing. When he puts down the last page we both sit there and it gets real quiet for a while.

Finally I can see he's not gonna do much talking so I look over and ask him, "Well, Steve? What do you think?"

"It's a fine story, Billy," he tells me. "I'm glad you let me see it." Only he's not even looking at me.

"Look, Steve," I said. "That's not what I gave it to you for. I don't care about none o' that, you know that."

He gets up and starts walking up and down a while.

"Well?" I ask him again.

"All right, Billy," he says after a while. "I know that isn't the reason you asked me to read your—your story. But—all right, what do you expect me to say?"

"Anything you wanna say," I tell him.

He looks at me and then he stops walking up and down and comes over and stands right in front of me.

"All right," he says. And now he's looking me right in the eye and I'm kinda expecting to hear something, know what I mean? "All I can tell you, Billy," he says, "is that I don't feel involved."

"That's a kinda funny way to talk, Steve," I tell him. "In-volved—I didn't ask you if you're involved. Anyhow, what do you mean by that exactly, mind tellin' me in plain Eng-lish? Cause I don't know if I dig what you mean by in-volved."

He sits down and starts talking a whole lot of double-talk and he's using all kinds of fancy words about how he don't

see how he can go into this any further without going into a
lot of recriminations and a discussion of the ramifications
and psychological motivations and all kinds of crap like that
and pretty soon I can't even tell what the hell he's talking
about except I got a pretty good idea he don't exactly know
either so that makes us even right there I guess.

"Hey, Steve," I finally butt in. "Look. Whyn't we keep it
nice and simple?"

He gives me a kinda funny look but I look right back at
him real dumb and finally he looks away.

"Okay, Billy," he says. "Let's put it this way then. Let's
say this is only one small part of the story—is that simple
enough?"

"Sure, that's real cool," I tell him. "Like you mean it is
true far as it goes—that it, Steve?"

"W-e-l-l," he says, "I don't know whether I'd put it just
that way, Billy. Truth is a damned complicated thing, especially when you're trying to pin it down in language. This
story, as you've written it, is twisted quite a bit. Or slanted,
I suppose would be closer to what I'm trying to say. For
example, the way you've got it, it would seem Betsy and
I were divorced because of what she says about me—
whereas that's not the real reason at all."

"Good enough," I tell him. "Can you tell me what the real
reason was then—I mean, if it ain't that."

He looks down at the floor and his voice gets real low so I
gotta listen kinda hard.

"The real reason," he says, talking real sad, like he don't
like having to say this—"the real reason Betsy and I were
divorced, Billy, is that she lied to me for over ten years—or,
if you prefer to put it another way, she refused to tell me the
truth about herself. Which, as far as I'm concerned, is the
same as lying."

I looked at him for a little while. He was still staring down
at the floor like he was trying to find something down there.
I'm just sitting there kinda thinking over what he's just told

me. But then all of a sudden something makes like a little *click* in my head.

"Fair enough, Steve," I tell him. "Now can I ask you just one more thing?"

"Of course you can," he says.

"Well," I tell him, "it's not that I care so damn much about Betsy in all this, you understand—but I'm trying to figure why she should of lied to you all that time, or not tell you the truth about herself, like you say, without you didn't make it look to her like that'd be a hell of a sight better'n *tellin'* you the truth right off the bat. Can you maybe straighten me out on that one, Steve?"

He looks up and opens his mouth to talk but only one word comes out.

"Well," he says and then he closes his mouth again. That's all he says.

I wait a while and then I see there ain't gonna be nothing much more outa him.

"Okay," I tell him. "That's what I kinda thought. And you know somethin'? I always did know you were a hell of a big man in the word department, Steve, but goddamn if I ever would of believed anybody could tell me as much as you just did with that one little word, you know that?"

After that neither one of us don't say anything else for quite a while. What's the use of anybody saying anything? What the hell, the both of us know exactly how we stand, don't we?

So finally I tell him it's getting pretty late and I gotta catch a little shut-eye on account of I got kind of a rough day ahead of me tomorrow.

He digs, all right, and he gets up and starts to go to the door. I go with him and hold the door open while he puts on his coat and hat.

When he gets out in the hall he says, "Well, so long, Billy."

"No, pal," I tell him. "You got it wrong this time. Not so

long—goodbye," and I close the door on him and go back into the living room and sit down and think for a long time before I finally hit the sack.

Sure, I guess he's nothing but a no-good bastard. I don't s'pose anybody'd give me much of an argument about that without they're the same kinda bastard themself, which I guess maybe there's probably quite a few of 'em around nowadays at that. And as far as Betsy goes—well, seems to me she's damn near as bad as Steve, if not maybe even worse in some ways. Sure, I can see where she might of had lots of reasons why she never told him about herself, way she was brought up and all like that. But still and all is that a good excuse? Cause if it is, where's anybody gonna stop when it comes to making excuses for damn near anything? Cause okay, take a guy like Steve. What is he, when you come right down to it, but a guy who's like twisted in the head from the way he's been brought up, right? So how the hell can *he* help himself, if that's the answer. What the hell, he ain't the first one to come up with the idea that the Jews are all no goddamn good, that's for sure. There's plenty of guys around just like him—and from all I can see it don't look to me like brains got much to do with it either, cause lots of 'em got all the brains anybody needs, if it comes to just thinking being much use, know what I mean?

Which right there's the part of this I don't even like to think about at all. Dig?

Whodunit

Whodunit

The moment we were off the air I left the control room and went up to the sponsor's booth. I knew it had gone bad.

Oh well, I thought, Jim will understand. He's been through it himself often enough, God knows. Anyway he can't blame me for it; the script read all right. He approved it himself. What an idiotic business . . . The hell with it.

Jim looked up at me as I walked in. His eyebrows were raised and he had that faintly amused expression on his face. I knew that expression. I knew it only too well. Anyway, I told myself again, this time he can't blame me. Let him blame anybody he wants to—from the director right down through the entire cast; just so I'm out from under. I'm sick of the whole mess. Every damn week it starts all over again. Every seven days, and always the same problems. Well boys, what's it gonna be this time—who do we knock off this week and who done it and why and how does he get caught and by whom? Those endless, miserable script conferences, those dreary casting discussions, those interminable sessions with director, set designer, camera-crew—

"Well, Bob," Jim said as I sank into an upholstered chair beside him.

"Yes, Jim," I looked at him disgustedly, "I know, I know. Pretty rotten, huh?"

"Sort of—ah—gamey," he said with that thin smile of his. "Had kind of a high odor." His face sobered. "We're going to have to do something, Bob," he went on. "I don't know just what but we're definitely going to have to do something, laddie."

"Great," I said unenthusiastically. I never knew what to expect next when he started calling me laddie. "Any suggestions?" I asked a bit sourly.

He took his time about answering. His eyes focussed on some point over my left shoulder. He pursed his lips. The tips of his fingers came together and formed the familiar cage. I sat and waited for the pronouncement, trying to appear unconcerned.

We were alone in the booth. Through the glass I watched the crew break down the set, packing away the debris of that night's fiasco, sober-faced men in grey porter's uniforms, pushing, hauling, shoving. At the far end of the stage several of the actors were holding the usual post-mortem. Archie Morrison glanced up over his shoulder toward us, then swiftly glanced away. He reminded me of the White Rabbit and I had an image of him suddenly scuttling off and popping down some dark hole before anybody could tell him how badly he had stunk up the airwaves tonight. He was evidently explaining something in great detail to Eve Benson, the girl he had just strangled for the entertainment and edification of the television audience. Eve watched with polite interest but all at once she yawned and covered her mouth with her hand.

"Not exactly suggestions," Jim's voice brought me back. "But I think we ought to have a serious talk, Bob. I have a feeling the whole show is getting just a little—ah—shall we say, stale? Maybe we ought to have a discussion about the basic format. Seems to me we're about due for a bit of a shakeup. Agreed?"

He was looking directly at me now. I returned his look and shrugged elaborately.

"Anything you say, Jim," I told him. "You're still head man. Whatever you think."

He stood up, flashed his white teeth in a dazzling smile, reached for his topcoat.

"Suppose we start with a few drinks," he said as I got to my feet and stood beside him. "We can talk better away from here."

He started briskly out of the booth with me trailing. It seemed to me at that moment that I was always trailing behind him, that I had been trailing him almost from the first time we met. I was beginning to get a bit tired of trailing Jim Peterson after some eight or nine years of it. But as I thought that, I also knew I would undoubtedly go right on unless something pretty drastic came along to shake me out of it.

I got my coat and hat and we left the building. It was cold outside. We walked about a block and a half without either of us saying much. He was heading east and I went along with him—as usual.

"Where we going?" I suddenly asked. "Not Cherio's, I hope."

He turned his crew-cut head toward me and smiled that bright, tooth-paste-ad smile of his.

"No, not Cherio's," he said. "Why? Why not Cherio's, you hope?"

"No special reason," I said. "I just wondered where we were heading, I didn't really mean it was important one way or the other."

"I thought you sounded a bit jaded," he laughed. "Cherio's," and he laughed again. "Same old mob, I suppose?"

"Yeah," I said. "Pretty much the same old mob, I guess."

"How do they stand it? Night after night after night, week

in, week out." He shook his head. "Good God! Those same dusty faces with all those tired clichés coming out of them. I wonder what it must feel like to have to go on and on and on like that.

"With nothing on earth to think about but next week's show?" I prompted.

"Something of the sort," he nodded.

"Pity the poor teevee wage slave," I said. "Television producers of the world unite—you have nothing to lose but your programs."

"Don't be bitter, laddie," Jim laughed. "Why be bitter? It's a living."

"Don't get me wrong, Jim," I told him. "Hell, I'm the original I-love-life boy."

"The soap, you mean? You plugging the competition?"

"No, not the soap, and definitely not the competition," I grinned. "Just the life is all."

"Quite a life," he agreed. "Yep, quite a life all right."

We reached Park Avenue and he turned into it and headed uptown.

"Where we going?" I asked again as I walked along beside him.

"I thought we might as well go on up to my place," he said. "We can talk quietly there and I've got as good booze as any other place in town. All right with you?"

"Sure," I told him. "It's O.K. with me."

Actually, it wasn't exactly O.K. I would have preferred some quiet bar, some place more impersonal. I had not been in Jim's apartment for over a year. Not since the accident, in fact. And while I did feel a sort of macabre curiosity about what the place would feel like without Ginny there, I wasn't so curious that I would not rather have gone somewhere else. I had always liked Ginny, though I never got to know her too well; and now that she was dead I found it a little hard to understand why Jim went on living there. After all, it had been her apartment before they got married and it seemed odd to me that a man would go on living in a place which must constantly remind him of his dead wife—especially when you think of the way she died.

It had happened about a year ago, when Jim and Ginny had been on their way to spend a weekend with some friends who lived upstate. According to the newspaper reports, they had taken a motor trip up into the Catskills where, while they were looking at the view from the top of a cliff in front of the old Catskill House, Ginny had slipped and fallen to her death. There had been a certain amount of fuss in the papers; and for a short time there was even some veiled gossip to the effect that there might be more to the accident than met the eye. But of course it eventually died down, since the only reason for gossip was the simple fact that Ginny had been a very rich girl, if that is a reason—which I suppose it could be at that.

At any rate, when Jim came back to town it was quite obvious that he was deeply affected by the tragedy. He and Ginny had always appeared terribly fond of each other so it didn't surprise me too much when he went off on an epic binge immediately after the funeral. Jim had never been much of a drinker before that, and I sort of stood by and helped him through it somehow despite the fact that while it was going on I also had to get the show on the air pretty much by myself for a couple of weeks.

Right here is as good a place as any to explain about the show. It was Jim's show to begin with; the whole idea of it was his. Jim and I had been friends for quite a while now, ever since I first got acquainted with him during World War II. At that time he was a colonel in the Signal Corps, in charge of a communications department at Noumea, New Caledonia, where I served as his Section Chief for eighteen months. Jim was some nine years older than I but we sort of hit it off right from the start. Later, after the war, when he became the producer of a highly successful radio show called *Suspicion* he gave me a job as his "assistant." I had always been interested in radio and I was grateful for the opportunity to learn something about it. In the beginning I suppose I was not really of very much use on the program but as time went on and I began to learn the ropes Jim leaned on me more and more. I was soon doing everything from turning out occasional scripts to helping with directorial and production chores, and after a couple of years it got to the point where I could reasonably flatter myself that I would not have been the easiest person on the show for him to replace.

When television began to become the important advertising medium and it became time to switch over, there were all sorts of problems to thrash out. Not many successful radio programs were able to survive the transition from sound alone to sound-plus-vision; *Suspicion* was one of the few which not only survived but became one of the top rating shows in the new medium. That put Jim smack up into the genius category right off the bat; and pretty soon he was the fair-haired boy around the Madison Avenue crowd. There were a few early attempts on the part of rival agencies and networks to duplicate the *Suspicion* formula but none of them were anything but abortive. This was not a matter of pure luck. I was right in the midst of it during the entire period and I can state without reservation that Jim Peterson always knew exactly what he was about; and the deceptively simple formula through which *Suspicion* was able to retain its original audience and build up an even larger following on television was one he had originated and maintained through a lot of hard, foot-slogging work. In his own special way Jim was one of the cleverest men I have ever known. Any man would have to be clever to go on turning out show after show as he did, every one of them based on nothing more than a deceptively simple premise and yet each one containing that particular little twist—or gimmick, as these things have come to be called—which stamped it unmistakably as a James Peterson production.

The whole idea of *Suspicion*, as anyone knows who owns a television set, is the element of humor that underlies every show. No matter how involved or even downright gruesome the actual plots might be—and some of them are very gruesome indeed—Jim always insisted on this undertone of sardonic humor: gallows humor, if you will, but nevertheless humor. I suppose that sounds simple enough too but believe me, it isn't.

Getting back though: a few months after Ginny died Jim told me he was quitting the show. It came as quite a shock to me; after all, *Suspicion* had been a major part of my life over the past six years. But when he calmly added that this meant that I would have to take over the show, handle the whole thing by myself, I was stunned. (I forgot to mention earlier that *Suspicion* was sponsored by Virginia Warren, Inc. and that Virginia Warren, Inc. was Ginny's cosmetics business and that she and Jim had got married about the same time Virginia Warren, Inc. bought the show when it was first kinescoped and shown around to prospective sponsors. In fact, their marriage under these circumstances was one of the main reasons for some of the gossip I mentioned earlier, particularly when it was announced, after Ginny's funeral, that Jim was taking over as the new head of Virginia Warren, Inc. Of course I knew how stupid all this vicious gossip was because I knew Jim had been more or less formally engaged to Ginny when I first met him; that is, if you can call a thing like that an engagement. Agreement, I suppose, might be a better word; for in the first place Ginny was already married at the time—though she and her former husband had already decided to get divorced as soon as he got out of the Air Force—and in the second place, since it might have caused a lot of unpleasant talk, neither Jim nor Ginny ever told many people about their plans until after her divorce came through.)

So there was Jim, running a television program and married to the sponsor—quite a switch in itself. And now here he was turning the show over to me, making me the producer of it, you see, with him becoming the new sponsor. All of which, I think you'll agree is jumbled up enough for anybody.

Well, to bring all this up to date now, I accepted the job and we drew up the contracts and that was that. Or rather, it seemed to be that; until I began to see what I had let myself in for. Within a few months I learned that there is an immense difference between handling a show under the supervision of the man who originated it and knows exactly what he wants it to be—even handling it alone for two or three weeks at a time as I had when Jim had to take some time off now and then because Ginny liked trips and insisted on his accompanying her whenever she went on one—anyway, there is an enormous difference between that kind of a job and the one it turns out to be when you're running the whole shebang all by yourself. So that by the end of that first year I was beginning to wonder whether I hadn't taken on more than I could handle.

But each time I brought this up Jim merely laughed it off and told me I was doing a fine job and to stop worrying about it. I tried my best but somehow it wasn't enough. Pretty soon I began to run into trouble of one sort or another. One time it would be a weak script—by now I was too busy to work with the writers as much as I had when Jim was there to run the show; another week it would be someone in the cast who would unexpectedly louse up a whole show by either muffing a line (these were the days of "live" shows, the pre-tape days) or forgetting a crucial piece of business, or some other idiotic thing no one could possibly foresee. One thing after another went wrong and it was beginning to get me down. I was getting stale and there seemed to be nothing I could do about it. I knew of no one I could turn the show over to for a short time; and each week I would somehow get through it only to face the next week's show with an absolutely blank mind. After a while I found myself dreading the prospect of next week's program and filled with a kind of dull horror at the persistent thought that at any moment the whole thing might simply fall apart.

Finally I went to Jim in desperation and tried to tell him what was going on. He was very sympathetic and friendly, as always. He let me finish and then told me that things were running quite smoothly for him at the moment and perhaps he could spare enough time to give me a hand. I begged him to scout around and see if he couldn't find some producer to take the program over for a while but he told me he was altogether out of touch after all this time and for the love of Pete to quit worrying, everything was going to turn out O.K.

That was when he first started coming around every week. And now, after three or four weeks with Jim in the sponsor's booth and having to go up there and re-hash the whole thing with him after each show, I found that instead of his presence being a help it actually made things worse than ever.

Tonight had been the worst of all. It seemed as if everything had gone haywire. Actors blew up in the middle of lines, sound cues were muffed—the whole thing was one long half-hour nightmare. I was ready to chuck the whole business and go off where I would not have to see or hear anything or anybody connected with television and lick my wounds in peace.

Instead of that, here we were now on our way to Jim's apartment to discuss "the basic format."

After we got settled and had a couple of drinks apiece I decided to tell him exactly how I felt. This time I had to convince him. Jim Peterson was never easy to convince but I knew I had to do it. While I tried to figure out just how to go about it so that he would not be able to talk me out of it again, I sipped my drink and looked around. Jim sat quietly on the sofa opposite me. Neither of us spoke for a little while and once again it occurred to me to wonder why he went on living here. Somehow the apartment seemed to retain Ginny's presence—the whole place made you think of her. Only now it had a sort of decorated look, whereas when she had lived here it had all seemed to "go with" her. Ginny had been an odd girl, with very definite tastes and opinions, but she had been very pleasant and cordial with me and I had always liked her well enough, from what little I saw of her.

These were random thoughts but I suppose my mind was more or less occupied with them, for when Jim spoke I gave a slight start.

"Sorry, Jim," I said. "Guess I must have been woolgathering or something. What did you say?"

He gave me an amused look.

"I asked whether you weren't about ready for a refill," he told me. "Your glass looks sort of empty."

"No, this'll be enough, thanks just the same," I said. "Look, Jim, I want to talk to you about something."

"Shoot," he said.

"I'm sorry," I began. "But I—"

"I know," he said before I could go on. "I know, Bob. You want to quit—isn't that it?"

"No, not exactly." I tried to tell him again that I only wanted to get away for a short rest. "Not for very long, actually. It's only that I feel I'm not doing the job I ought to and—well, you know."

"No, I don't know," he said. "I don't know at all. But I'd like to know. Why do you really want to get away?"

He was watching me as he spoke. There was a smile on his face but it seemed to me he was examining me very intently.

"I don't quite understand," I said. "Why should it be so hard to accept the fact that I'm pooped and need a little rest? Why should there have to be any more than that?"

"*I* didn't say there was any more than that," he said, still looking right into my eyes.

"Well then?"

He didn't answer. Now he got up and walked over to fix himself another drink.

"All right, Bob," he suddenly said, "I understand how you feel. How long do you want?"

"You mean it's O.K.?" I couldn't believe my ears. "I can take off for a little while?"

"Of course you can," he said. "Why not?"

Again I had the idea he was watching me narrowly, as if he were trying to note my slightest reactions, but I could not understand why he should be so interested as all that. I dismissed it as something I was only imagining.

"Well, that's a relief," I said. "Here I've been racking my brains trying to figure out how I was going to talk you into it and all I had to do was ask."

I grinned across at him. He merely sat there looking at me with a sort of quizzical expression in his eyes.

"What's up, Jim?" I asked after a moment.

"Nothing. Not a thing. Just trying to figure out something, that's all."

"Anything I can help with?"

For a few seconds he sat silently, looking off over my shoulder.

"Come to think of it," he finally said, "you're just the fellow who *can* help me. That is, if you'll do it . . ."

"Well go ahead," I said when he stopped. "What do you want me to do?"

"Actually very little," he said after another pause. "Very, very little. But it's damned important to me."

"Well go on and tell me. What do you want?"

"The truth. All I want is the truth, Bob," he said evenly, looking straight into my eyes.

"I don't know what this is all about," I laughed embarrassedly, "but I'll tell you what I can as truthfully as I can."

"That's good enough. But before I ask you anything about —before I ask you to tell me anything, it's only right that I tell *you* a few things. . . . For instance, about that—ah—so-called accident of Ginny's, to start with. You needn't look at me like that, laddie. I'm not off my rocker. Ginny never fell off that cliff . . . I pushed her over."

I stared at him, vaguely aware of the dead silence that followed his last words—but for several moments my mind simply refused to accept the meaning of what he had just told me. He sat there nodding his head at me gravely, almost solemnly, with his eyes fixed on mine as if he were waiting for my reaction to some casual remark he had just made. It was almost as if he had been discussing some completely objective matter which scarcely concerned him, rather than . . .

"What the hell is all this about?" I burst out. "You're not seriously trying to tell me that—"

"Oh yes, Bob. I'm very serious." His eyes flicked away now and went back to looking at some spot over my shoulder.

"Well what the hell are you telling *me* about it for?" I almost shouted.

"You're my friend, Bob," he said. His eyes came back to mine again then darted away almost immediately. "You're my best friend. Who else does a fellow talk to about something like this if not his best friend?"

"Ah, you're kidding," I said. I leaned back in my chair and looked at him. "Come on, Jim—what's this all about?"

He smiled bleakly.

"I'm trying to tell you—if you'll listen," he said.

"How the hell do you expect me to hold still for anything as crazy as this, for God's sake? Come on—quit it, will you?"

"What's the trouble, Bob? Don't you believe me?"

"Come on now," I said again. "Quit it. Of course I don't believe you."

He shrugged and let out a little laugh.

"Well in that case I suppose there's no point in my going on with it, is there?"

I looked at him. He seemed quite serious.

"Listen," I said. "Just for the sake of the gag—whatever it is—suppose I go along with you for a minute. All right, let's say you're telling the truth. Not that I believe it, understand. But, all right, suppose you are. Now why the hell would you tell me about it? After all," I forced a grin, "I haven't made any promises not to repeat it. And even though I am your friend, still that doesn't mean I'd want to be put in a spot where I'd have to shield a fellow who's—well, committed murder is the phrase, isn't it?"

"Yes, that's the phrase," he said gravely. "But about putting you in any spot—I was just coming to that. Look, laddie, don't get the idea I don't know what I'm saying. And about your having to worry about shielding anybody, forget it. There's not a thing you can do about it. You don't think I'd ever admit having told you any of this, do you?" He broke off and laughed.

"But still—why *tell* me then and expect me to keep quiet about it?"

"You're not bound to anything," he said. "Nothing to stop you from telling anybody you want to . . . Only you may as well get this straight right away. First place nobody'll believe you—where's your proof? Second place I've already told you I'd most certainly deny it if it ever came up—in which case people'd no doubt end up thinking you're batty. So I can't quite see what you're going to be able to do about it no matter how it goes—whether you end up believing me or not." He stopped and looked blandly over at me. "Do *you?*"

"I see what you mean," I said slowly. "You may be right at that . . . Of course, I could always write it and use it on the show, couldn't I? Sounds like it ought to make a pretty fair script, don't you think?"

"Go ahead and try it," he said, smiling crookedly. "But I don't think it'll be any good. Some of the subject matter's too tough."

"Hell, we can always find a way to iron out the rough spots, you know that," I said.

"Perhaps," he said. "Perhaps you can but I strongly doubt it."

"Well—I suppose you know best."

He gave me a peculiar look.

"You have no idea," he said. "Wait'll you hear the whole

thing." He shook his head. "*Uh*-uh—you'd never get away with it on television. Too touchy. Like to hear it?"

"I sure as hell would," I said, not quite certain now what to believe but beginning to feel uneasy in spite of myself.

"Fine," he said. "In that case, laddie, I wouldn't dream of holding out on you. I've already told you—or haven't I?—you're the best friend I've got in the world. Fellow can't hold out on his best friend, can he?"

There was something peculiar about the way he kept repeating the words, but I could not put my finger on it. There was nothing in his expression to help me out. He just sat there, blandly returning my look.

"O.K., Jim," I said. "I'm still waiting."

"Fine," he said again. He paused, looked me in the eye for a long moment, then turned his head to stare out the window. "Remember when we first met, Bob?"

"Why, yes, of course I do. Noumea, nineteen forty-three. Why?"

"Well, it's a sort of involved script, but that's when you came into it. You probably don't remember it, but there was one night when we both got a little loaded and drove out to Ton Touta and then drank a lot more and while I was good and drunk I told you about Ginny for the first time. Perhaps you've forgotten it but—"

"No," I said. "I haven't forgotten it. I remember that night very well."

"You do," he said, rather than asked. He gave me a swift glance, then looked away again. "I wasn't sure whether you'd remember. You know, I've thought about that night lots of times since then." He sounded as if he were talking to himself. "Pretty crazy night, wasn't it?"

"Yes, I guess it was," I said. "I've thought of it a number of times since then myself."

It certainly was a pretty crazy night. The whole thing began when Jim asked me what I was doing that evening.

We were having dinner at the officers' mess. The food, as usual, was God-awful. It was a hot evening and I had been sitting there sweating and wishing I were almost anyplace but where I was. I had only been in Noumea for about a week or so but I was already good and sick of it by that time; so when Jim asked me if I felt like taking a drive out to the air base at Ton Touta, some twenty-five miles out of town, I told him I'd be glad to. There wasn't a hell of a lot to do around Noumea of an evening in those days—not that I suppose there's a hell of a lot to do there nowadays, as far as that goes.

After dinner I went along with him over to his quarters.

"I've got a fifth of Canadian Club stashed in my foot locker," he told me as we walked down the dusty street. "Friend of mine flew it in from New Zealand a few days ago and I've been saving it. Out here the stuff is considered liquid gold, you know."

"So I've heard," I grinned at him. "My God! Canadian Club—must be nice being a colonel."

"Oh, it has certain advantages," he laughed. "But look here, let's forget this rank crap tonight and just pretend we're a couple of plain Joes. I'm a bit tired of being a colonel right this minute."

"Well, I guess I can afford to quit being a captain if you're willing to quit being a colonel," I told him. "Sir," I added.

"O.K.," he said. "And suppose we start by dropping the sir business, all right?"

"I was only kidding," I said.

He looked over at me.

"I see," he said and broke into a pleasant smile. "Funny— guess I've forgotten what it feels like to be kidded." He shook his head.

"I suppose colonels don't get too much kidding at that, do they?"

"Not a hell of a lot. You probably don't realize it but you're a lot better off as a captain."

I remained tactfully silent.

"You don't believe that, I guess," he said.

"Well . . ."

We both laughed.

"It's true though," he said, sounding suddenly very boyish as he grinned at me. "Seriously, it is, Bob."

It was the first time he had called me by my first name and it sounded strange. He seemed somewhat embarrassed himself; but I pretended not to notice.

"Well, I'll try and take your word for it," I said, "since I don't suppose I'll ever be in a position to know through personal experience, colonel."

"Not colonel," he said. "Jim's the name."

"All right," I said. "Jim."

When we got to his quarters he dug down into his foot locker and came up with a sure-enough bottle of Canadian Club. It hadn't even been opened; but we soon fixed that. We sat around for a half-hour or so and polished off better than half the bottle. And while we drank we talked. I asked him what he had done before getting into the army and he said he'd been in advertising for the past ten years and had just got into the production end of radio before the war broke out. We talked about all sorts of things, mostly what it had been like before the army and how we hoped things would be after we got back into civilian life again—the usual sort of thing two fellows might talk about under those circumstances, though at first it was pretty impersonal. I told him I had always wanted to get into radio myself and he said something about looking him up after the war and maybe he'd be able to help me out—"That is if I ever manage to get back into it myself by that time"—and I said O.K., I might take him up on that one of these days.

By the time we finished half the bottle we were both feeling all right. Also by now we were becoming a good bit less impersonal. Finally he said we might as well get out of there and go over to the motor pool and pick up a jeep. I said it was O.K. with me and off we went.

On the way out to Ton Touta in the jeep we kept on taking belts at the bottle. It was nice and cool with the top down. About ten miles out of Noumea it began to rain but we kept going without bothering to put the top up. After a while it stopped raining and now the dust was settled on the dirt road. We wound along through occasional groves of palm trees and overhead the stars hung in the sky like fireflies and by now we were both feeling no pain at all. For the first time since arriving in New Caledonia I began to feel a little less homesick. I was beginning to like Jim Peterson and by this time I had completely forgotten about his being a colonel. He was a nice guy, that was all, and I had enough Canadian Club under my belt not to care whether he saw I thought so or not and everything was rosy and I was glad I was here, rather than up north on one of those hell-holes like Guadal or Iwo having the hell pasted out of me by the Japs.

Pretty soon the bottle was dead. We chucked it into a patch of woods we were passing. I looked over at Jim.

"How you doing?" I asked.

"Fine," he said. "I'm O.K. You all right?"

"Couldn't be better. You able to drive all right?"

"Nothing to it," he said, glancing over at me. "Not worried, are you?"

"Me?" I laughed. "Hell no, I haven't got a care in the world. I wouldn't mind if we ended up in a ditch and had to sleep right here. In fact I can't think of a better place to spend the rest of this war than right here in this jeep."

"Well don't worry, son, I've got other plans. You're not going to spend the war in this."

"I was afraid of that," I laughed.

Presently we saw lights ahead. We made a turn off the main road through a gate, showed our ID cards to a sentry, and after we were passed through we wound along a dirt road for a few minutes. Buildings and quonsets began to loom up and get thicker and thicker on both sides of the road and in a little while we drew up alongside a greyish-looking ramshackle building which was all lit up. I could hear a jukebox booming inside. Jim stopped the jeep and cut the motor.

"Here we are," he said.

"What's this?"

"Officers' club," he said, climbing out of the jeep. "Come on, I know somebody here who'll probably be able to spare another jug. We can use another one."

"Canadian Club again?" I got out and started toward the front door of the building with him.

"I hope," he said, holding up two crossed fingers.

"Oh for the life of a colonel," I said.

"I told you it had certain advantages."

"You also told me I was better off being a captain, remember?"

"Now where the hell do you suppose I ever picked up a silly notion like that, I wonder," he grinned as we went in.

"Don't look at *me*," I said. "How would I know? I'm nothing but a captain who just came along for the ride."

"Some ride," he said, looking at me and laughing.

"What's the matter?" I asked.

"Here, take a look at yourself." He pointed to the mirror behind the bar were we were now standing.

I looked and began laughing myself. My face was all streaked with dust and my hair was standing up on end like some kind of a fright-wig. Somewhere along the line I had taken off my overseas cap and stuffed it into my back pocket.

"I better do something about this," I said. "Where's the can?"

He pointed toward it and I went in and washed my face and combed my hair. When I came out he was talking to someone at the bar, a tall man with iron-grey hair. When I got over there I saw it was a major. Jim introduced us and the major pardoned himself and went off.

"I'll see if I can dig one up," he said as he left.

"What's this?" I asked Jim. "More liquid gold?"

"Just watch," he said with a broad wink. "I told you I've got a drag, son."

"Boy, if that guy comes back with another jug of Canadian Club, I'm afraid I'm going to have to ignore your advice and start bucking for colonel anyway."

"All right, but when you make it don't say I didn't warn you."

"Fair enough," I said.

A few minutes later we were out in the jeep again with a brand new bottle of Canadian Club. No doubt about it, there certainly were distinct advantages in being a colonel. During the next few hours I may have told him so several hundred times more but by then I had drunk enough so that I could not remember very much of anything I told him. However, I had no trouble remembering some of the things he told me during the rest of that night.

Most of them had to do with Ginny. Virginia Warren, that is—and I remember how queer it sounded to me when he told me who it was. For of course I had heard the name. Only it seemed strange to have a man tell you about his girl and then to learn that her name was one you'd always thought of as a sort of trade mark rather than an actual name belonging to a real flesh-and-blood woman. It was almost like hearing someone say he was in love with Ivory Soap or Chanel No. 5 or—well, Elizabeth Arden, is more like it, I suppose.

Anyway, before we finally made our way back to Noumea and somehow wound up in our separate quarters Jim had told me a lot about Ginny Warren.

She sounded like quite a girl.

According to his description she was: "Tall, about five eight. Honey blonde, built like a brick privy and dresses like a Hattie Carnegie model. Not quite beautiful but pretty damn close to it and certainly not far enough from it so anybody'd worry about it."

There was a good deal more along the same lines, most of it sounding like the sort of thing any homesick soldier might have told you about "the girl back home"; but it seemed to me I detected a certain proprietary note underneath all this rhapsodizing. Of course we were both good and loaded by the time he got on the subject of Virginia Warren, Inc. Even so I remember that at one point I had the curious impression of listening to a man gloating over some valuable possession rather than nostalgically describing the woman he was supposedly in love with. However, since it was none of my business in the first place—and besides it was difficult to think clearly with all that Canadian Club under my belt—I more or less disregarded that part of it.

"She sounds pretty wonderful, Jim," I said after he finished telling me how clever she was and how she had built up her immensely successful cosmetics business "from nothing but a small stake, you understand, with practically no help from anybody at all," as he kept repeating—almost as though he were trying to convince himself rather than explain something to me. "She sounds pretty wonderful—why didn't you marry her before you left the States? I mean after all, a gal like that must have a lot of guys after her. You say she loves you too, so as long as you both figure on getting married, why didn't you do it before leaving?"

"We would have," he said. "Except for one small problem. Ginny's already married."

"Oh," I said. "I see,"

"No you don't," he said, shaking his head. "It's nothing like that, Bob. She and her husband are—ah—separated. They were going to be divorced anyway. He's Sherman Warren—ever hear of him?"

"The Main Line character with all the moolah?" I asked. "You mean *the* Sherman Warren—the polo-player character?"

"That's the guy," Jim said. "He's the one who gave Ginny the stake to start her business on and naturally she feels sort of obligated to him."

"Well for God's sake," I said, "that doesn't seem like much of a reason to stay married to a guy if she's not in love with him. Hell, from what I hear of Sherman Warren he's got about two-thirds of all the money in the world and probably owns a piece of White Christmas besides."

Jim laughed and I told him it wasn't my gag but something I'd been told Joe Frisco once said about Andrew Mellon—only when Joe said it he had said Melancholy Baby instead of White Christmas, which for all I know, might be worth even more.

He laughed again and then went on to say that there was another reason Ginny had not divorced Warren.

"Point is," he said, "Warren joined the Royal Air Force about two years ago. He's over in North Africa or some place right now and Ginny felt it would look sort of nasty if she were to divorce him while he's still overseas, even though he'd already consented to it."

"Yes—well, of course that does kind of make it tough."

"Oh well," he shrugged. "Anyway, as soon as he comes home she's going through with it and as soon as that's over with—that is if I ever get out of this in one piece—we'll be married."

"And live happily ever after?"

"What do you mean?" he gave me a quick look.

"Nothing much," I said. "Just kidding—pretty corny, I guess."

His face relaxed in an embarrassed grin.

"Sorry," he said. "Didn't mean to sound touchy. I guess you're right, Bob, colonels don't get much kidding. I'm probably out of the habit of it."

I can't remember just when it was that he began to tell me some of the more personal things about Ginny Warren. I do know that I tried to stop him at one point—figuring he was by then so drunk he didn't realize what he was saying and might be sorry he'd spoken so much once he sobered up. But it was no good trying to get him to stop. He was all wound up by then. Not only that but I had the feeling he'd been wound up for quite a while and had only been waiting for an opportunity to talk to someone about all this. It obviously was on his mind; and after I had heard it I could easily enough see why.

Apparently, in spite of the fact that he'd just finished building Ginny Warren up as the dream girl of the world, Jim himself was not entirely convinced that she was. Far from it. He was drunk enough now to let me in on some of the more intimate aspects of her character. It seemed he had certain suspicions that she had done a good bit of what he called "playing around" during the past few years. The thing that was troubling him was whether this was only due to her unhappy marriage to Sherman Warren—in which case, as he told me, he could understand it (though again he sounded more as if he were convincing himself rather than me)—or if it might not indicate a more basic flaw in her character . . .

"You see," he said, frowning slightly, "Ginny's a hell of a fine girl, warm-hearted and sweet and all that, but naturally, since she's made all this money by herself she's—oh, I don't know, I suppose you might say she's . . . ah . . . developed a mind of her own. I mean to say, she's not the kind of a girl who'd hold still for any man trying to tell her what to do— understand my point?"

"Yes, Jim, I understand," I told him, wishing I could get him to stop. "Look, it's getting pretty late, don't you think?"

"Oh, I suppose I'm just worrying about nothing," he went on, as if I had not spoken. "What the hell, I know her. Once we're married she'll settle down and everything'll be fine."

"Of course it will," I said. "Sure it will. Look, we've both got to be up pretty early. It's almost three o'clock. Maybe we ought to try and get a few hours sleep anyway, don't you think?"

Eventually we went back to Noumea and he dropped me off at my place. Just before I got out of the jeep he thanked me for listening to "all his problems." I laughed and told him it was O.K.

"No, but seriously," he said. "I appreciate it, Bob. You know, sometimes a fellow feels sort of like talking things out. Helps to get a kind of perspective—you understand?"

"Sure it does," I said. "Goodnight, Jim. See you in the morning."

He waved and drove off. I remember that he drove quite capably, drunk as he seemed to be.

Next morning, sometime before lunch, he took me aside and asked me whether he had pestered me too much the night before. "I'm awfully sorry," he said. "Guess I must have put away quite a bit of booze—more than I realized. I've never done much drinking before I got into this."

"Oh hell, you don't want to think about that," I reassured him. "We were both doing all right, I guess. Hell, I've still got half a load on right this minute."

"Well," he said, with a slightly worried look on his face, "I was just asking. I hope I didn't say anything—you know, out of line. Seems to me I must have said—ah—quite a bit about Ginny . . . didn't I?"

"No, you were O.K. You didn't say anything out of line."

He seemed to relax.

"It was kind of a good night at that, wasn't it?" he grinned at me. "I mean to say, I had a lot of fun."

"Me too," I said.

So that's how I first heard of Ginny Warren. As a woman, that is. Because as I said before, I had certainly heard of Virginia Warren, Inc. long before I ever met Jim Peterson.

Jim was looking at me over the rim of his glass. He took a long swallow of his drink, then put the glass down.

"Yes," he said. "Well. . . . Anyway. That was how you came into the picture, Bob."

"I don't quite understand what you mean by coming into the picture."

"Well, you remember when you got your orders to go back

to the States. By then we were pretty close friends, you remember, and I asked you to do me a favor when you got to New York."

"Yes, of course I remember. You asked me to look Ginny up and tell her I'd been out there with you and so on. Which I did, as you know."

I waited for him to go on but he said nothing and I glanced up and saw that he was still watching me.

"Point is," he said now, "there were a few other items about Ginny I never did mention to you. Main reason, of course, was that at that time I myself wasn't too sure. And besides, sometimes when a fellow's in love—or is trying to convince himself he's in love—he doesn't . . . ah . . . want to see things too clearly."

"Oh, I don't know," I said. "You gave me a pretty complete briefing on her in the time I was out there. Hell, by the time I saw her I felt as if I'd known her for years."

"Yes, I suppose you must have at that," he answered. "After you had lunch with her that first time, she wrote me a long letter. All about what a nice guy you were and how glad she was to see a buddy of mine. Buddy—hell of a word, isn't it? Remember, during the war—buddies?" He laughed. "But anyway, I felt pretty good about it when I got the letter. Then you saw her a couple of times after that and she wrote me about that too. After the third or fourth letter I still felt pretty good about it—only . . . ah . . . not quite as good as before, you understand. . . ."

"What the hell are you talking about, Jim?" I blurted out. "You don't mean to tell me you ever had any ideas about Ginny and me being anything but—"

"No—hold your horses, will you?" He grinned crookedly at me and waved his hand. "It's only that—well, you understand."

"I don't think I do, Jim," I said.

"Oh hell—doesn't matter anyway," he said. "Because I finally got back all right and then after the war Ginny got her divorce from Warren and we got married. Of course by that time I was already beginning to suspect she was a bit of a nympho but still that didn't seem to be any good reason not to go ahead and—"

"Jim! For Christ's sake!" I said. "Cut it out, will you? I don't want to hear any more of this."

He looked at me as if I had made some corny joke and suddenly he burst into a short, raucous laugh.

"You trying to pretend you never knew it?" he said. "If so, laddie, you're probably the only guy in New York who didn't." He laughed again. "You wouldn't try to kid me, now would you?"

I was still staring at him. So that was it! But even as the idea began to take shape in my mind I refused to have anything to do with it. How could he possibly suspect that Ginny and I had . . .

"Now look here, Jim," I said. "Let's get something straight, right now before you go any further."

"Why of course," he said blandly. "What's on your mind?"

"You know good and goddamn well what's on my mind," I said coldly. "No—wait a second. There's nothing funny about this. A joke's a joke but I can't see where this is anything to—"

"Oh, come on now," he interrupted. "Forget it." He waved his hand. "What's the matter with you?" He looked at me innocently. "I just thought perhaps you might've heard about it, that's all I meant."

"Where the hell would I be apt to hear anything like that, for God's sake?" I looked him straight in the eye, trying to make it sound convincing, but as a matter of fact I had heard some rather unpleasant rumors about Ginny from time to time over the past few years. Still, aside from that one night at Ton Touta Jim had never spoken of anything of this sort again, so I had more or less assumed that even if the rumors were true he knew nothing about them.

"O.K., O.K.," he was saying. "It was nothing, nothing at all. Didn't mean anything by it. Just one of those remarks. No reason to get excited."

I kept quiet and waited for him to go on. By this time, though, I was extremely nervous and tense.

"Well?" he now said. "Care to hear the rest of it?"

"Suit yourself," I shrugged. "If you feel there's any point in telling me. . . ."

"You may as well hear it," he said. "Why not?"

"O.K., go ahead—I'm listening."

Good enough, he said . . .

You see, after I'd been married to Ginny for about six months I discovered she had a tremendous sexual appetite. Practically insatiable. I also discovered I was by no means the only guy in town who knew that. Understand, I don't know if she was really a nympho. But I did find out she'd been—ah—pretty free and easy with a number of men over the past few years. And that apparently she saw no reason why marriage should prevent her from going right on with other men if she happened to meet any who . . . ah . . . appealed to her. Of course it wasn't as if I hadn't already half-known some of this before I married her. Only thing, I had no idea she'd carried it that far, you see.

Still, while I can't say I felt good about all this, I did my best to cope with it. Figuratively and literally . . . But it was no good, I couldn't make the grade. And after a year or so I began to understand why Sherm Warren'd been so amenable about the terms of the divorce—or at least I thought I understood. You know, he made quite a generous financial settlement with her even though he must have known she was damn well fixed herself. Point is, Ginny was enough to break a man's back! Any man—I don't care who he was. Or how young. . . .

Still, as I say, I did what I could. Even after I began to realize it was no use. And we went along that way for a few

years. Of course during that period Ginny behaved fairly
discreetly—by that I mean she didn't play around in New
York City very much. Perhaps not at all. You remember she
liked to take these trips here and there around the country? I
can't quite figure out why in hell she always insisted on my
tagging along, except possibly to have me on the spot so she
could humiliate me. Or something—I'm not quite sure what.
She was an extraordinary girl. Terribly complex personality,
never met anybody quite like her. However . . .

One night we got into a big hassle about . . . ah . . . well,
anyway—a big hassle. By that time everything was pretty
much out in the open between us, you understand, and we
were always brawling at each other like a couple of strange
bulldogs. Somewhere along the line I got out of control and
began calling her a common bitch and a cheap trollop and
several other highfalutin things like that. All the time I went
raving on she sat still and looked at me. Ginny had a way of
looking at you that could. . . . But she let me get all
through and then she asked me what I thought I was going
to do about it. That made me madder than ever and I *really*
started calling her names. Till all of a sudden she gave me
one of the nastiest smiles you've ever seen and reminded me
that I still hadn't mentioned what I thought I was going to
do about it. At which point I suppose I blew up altogether,
because without even thinking, I told her I was going to
divorce her.

Big mistake. . . .

Because you see, Bob, Ginny was no fool, whatever else
she may have been. Lots of ways I had to admire her, even
though I pretty much hated her guts by then. Yes sir, she
was quite a girl, Ginny was. Just about as clever as they
come. I really mean that, Bob—

"All right," I said. "Granted that she was a clever girl.
What's that got to do with me?"
"I'm coming to it," he said. "Don't crowd me. You'll see,

this script's got a few real kickers in it. And a wow of a finish too, wait'll you hear it."

"Well what do you say we start getting to it."

"I will, don't worry," he grinned. "No sense getting all worked up. We've got plenty of time."

"Whatever you say. You're the boss." I pointedly looked at my watch.

He ignored it and I began to get irritated.

"It's after midnight, Jim."

"It is?" he said politely. "Had no idea it was so late."

For one moment I thought of telling him to go to hell and walking out.

"Well?" He was looking at me and I had an uneasy feeling that he knew exactly what I was thinking and was amused by it. "Shall I stop now? Or would you care to hear the rest of this?"

"Go ahead." But I could not resist adding a petulant, "By all means."

He smiled and went on.

As I was saying, Bob, Ginny was a very bright girl. As soon as I told her I was going to divorce her she got right down to business.

"On what grounds?" she asked.

"Adultery," I answered. "What the hell other grounds do I need?"

She gave me that nasty little smile again and then asked me how I proposed going about proving it in court. And at that point I made my biggest mistake. I began bragging. Before I was through I told her all about having hired a private detective to check on her on several occasions over the past few months when I had had good reason to believe she was . . . ah . . . what is so delicately referred to as being indiscreet.

Stupid tactical error on my part. Absolutely idiotic, should have known better. Man ought never to tip his mitt when he's dealing with a sharp cooky like Ginny.

However. . . . All she did was light a cigarette and look up at me and start laughing.

"Why, Jim," she said. "I had no idea you were so efficient. But as long as you are I think it would be only friendly to give you a little hint of what you might be letting yourself in for."

I asked her what in hell she meant by that. And then she stopped laughing and let me in on her little plan. It was quite a plan—seems she'd had it in reserve for some time. She quietly informed me that she'd been aware of my suspi- cions—*suspicions*, for Christ's sake!—and that she'd known all along about my having had her trailed. Accordingly, she'd worked out a little scheme of her own in order to be able to deal with the situation—again her own words—if and when it arose.

This scheme of hers, like most strokes of pure genius, had the merit of extreme simplicity—almost obviousness. She would be perfectly willing to give me my freedom—as she called it. With, however, certain . . . ah . . . shall we say, qualifications. Mind you, Bob, all this came out of her as if she had it ready right along—as of course she had. In any case, here's all she wanted. Number one—I was to give her one hundred thousand dollars as a settlement. Naturally she knew I had nowhere near that amount of money, that is outside of what we had jointly—which of course was an- other matter. You see, part of her money was in a joint ac- count with mine. But she made it clear she's wasn't referring to that. Still, she said, she felt entitled to a good-sized finan- cial settlement since—as she carefully pointed out—a good part of my income ever since we'd been married had come out of her sponsoring my show. And when I mentioned the obvious fact that *Suspicion* would have been sponsored any- way, whether she'd bought it or not, she waved that aside as irrelevant.

The next thing she told me was that she would insist on divorcing *me*, that under no circumstances would she permit me to divorce her—that was out of the question. She simply wouldn't have it.

"How do you propose going about stopping me?" I asked her.

"Oh, I don't believe there will be any difficulty," she smiled.

"Well, just for the sake of the argument," I told her. "Because so far I'm afraid I can't go along with you. You see, my love, I happen to know of some three-quarters of a million in tax-free bonds you've got stashed away in a safe-deposit box at the Guaranty Trust—so I can't quite see myself handing you a hundred thousand I haven't got and don't expect to have in any ascertainable future. Now then—what makes you so sure you can convince me it would be a good idea to let you divorce me?"

"Oh, I think I can convince you, Jim," she laughed. Then she told me, still smiling, you understand, that she didn't have to have the hundred thousand in cash immediately—that she had enough to get along on all right—that actually the only reason she wanted it at all was to teach me a lesson because, as she said, she resented my having had her trailed. And then she gave me the following information.

Seems she had a boy friend, an immensely bright young lawyer who was apparently quite ready and willing to defend her in the event I tried to divorce her. She had already convinced him, I gathered, by . . . ah . . . certain methods of her very own, of the righteousness of her cause. He was quite prepared—with her expert testimony, naturally—to draw up a brief to the effect that, among other profound truths about my character, I was a member of the Communist party and had been for years and years. That she was divorcing me because I had made it impossible for her to go on living with me any longer by trying to force her to join the party and, failing that, insisting on her making large contributions to all sorts of unsavory and subversive causes. That I had threatened to beat her nightly unless she would read all sorts of unholy Communist pamphlets I had stashed away around the premises. And so forth and so on ad vomitum.

Very clever idea, don't you think? I thought so myself. Told her so right at the time. She seemed sort of pleased to hear it, matter of fact.

"But my God!" I sputtered. "She couldn't seriously have meant to go through with anything as ridiculous as that! Besides, that couldn't prevent you from divorcing her anyway."

"Of course not," he said. "I'm disappointed in you, Bob. Mean you don't get the plot?"

"I guess I do," I said slowly. "I guess I'm trying hard not to. Christ! I'm beginning to feel as if I'd just peered under a damp rock."

"You don't want to be so squeamish about a little thing like this," he laughed. "Hell, what's so nasty about a little situation between a man and wife. Besides, we haven't even got to the really interesting part yet. This is only the beginning. Subplot, more or less."

"I can hardly wait for the punch," I murmured.

"Of course it's too bad I've already given you the ending," he said. "Kills the suspense, I suppose."

"Don't worry about it," I told him. "It's got plenty of suspense."

He laughed.

"Thanks," he said, smiling benevolently and nodding as if I had just finished complimenting him on an actual script. "You know, I was beginning to think I'd lost my touch after all this time. You think it holds all right, do you?"

"Yes, Jim, it holds all right. . . . You understand, of course,"

I couldn't help adding, "there are a few weak spots here and there."

"Weak spots?" he said, raising his eyebrows. "Such as?"

"Well, for one thing," I began, "I don't believe a mere accusation of that kind could actually do you any real—"

"Why, Bob!" he interrupted. "I'm amazed."

"What's so amazing about it?" I said. "Sure, I know all about the black list. But still that doesn't mean a guy in your position, running one of the most successful shows in the business, would have to worry about being hurt just because someone says he's a member of—"

"Good Lord, Bob," he cut in, shaking his head with a sort of tolerant amusement.

But he did not smile as he continued.

"O.K.," he said. "Listen and maybe you'll learn something, chum. First place don't be a damn fool. What do you mean, *mere* accusation? Since when is an accusation of that sort mere, these days? Take a good look around you, laddie. You know how many people have been dropped. Why, all you have to do to anybody prominent in teevee today is point a finger at him. Who wants to know whether you can prove he's a red? Just make a big enough stink about him and—" drawing his forefinger across his throat, "—that's that. What difference does it make what he says after that? Who's going to listen? You know the term for people like that."

"All right," I said. "You mean 'controversial figure' . . . But my God! I still don't—"

"That's it," he said with a twisted smile. "Controversial figure—tidy little phrase, isn't it?"

I looked blankly at him for a few seconds. Suddenly an idea flashed across my mind. I tried to ignore it but I couldn't. Finally I said, "Look, Jim—I never thought of it before this, but—well, *did* you ever have anything to do with. . . . Oh, you know—politics?"

He did not answer immediately. He sat and looked steadily at me. After a few moments of it I began to get uneasy.

"Well, did you?" I asked.

"What do you think?"

"How would I know?" I shrugged embarrassedly. "I've never asked you about anything like this. I wouldn't ask you now, ordinarily—after all, it's none of my business—but since you're telling me all this—well, you know."

"In other words, you're not sure," he said evenly.

"Well how the hell can anybody be sure about a thing like that?"

"Even after all the years you've known me?" he said.

"Well, after all," I said uncomfortably, "I haven't any way of knowing how you feel about that sort of . . . Well how would I know, actually?"

Suddenly he laughed harshly.

"It's O.K., Bob. You don't have to squirm. Still, that ought to prove something or other." He let out a short laugh and shook his head. "Good Lord! Even you—after knowing me as well as you do and working as closely with me as you've done all these years—and you talk about mere accusations not being able to—"

"Listen," I cut in. "I never said I believed you were. All I did was ask."

"That's right," he said with that crooked smile. "All you did was ask. And you've never even heard anyone accuse me. And you've known me about as well as anyone in the business does. And all you've heard is what I've been telling you about a woman *merely*—" he laughed as he said the word, "—threatening to accuse me of something you've just been saying no one would ever believe because of a mere accusation! Mere! That's a hell of a word, when you get right down to it."

"Okay, Jim," I said. "I'm sorry."

"Why be sorry?" he said evenly. "See, I'll answer you. No—I'm not a Communist. No—I've never been a Communist, and just for the record, Ginny knew that too. But she also knew what it could mean to my career if she ever came out with a public accusation of that sort. She knew, and so do you, only you don't like to think about it—not that I blame you—that there's nobody on earth as wary as the man with a multi-million dollar business to protect. You take men like that—and that means your radio and television sponsors, the men who have the kind of advertising budgets that keep shows like *Suspicion* on the air—you go to people like that and just breathe a hint that the producer of a show they're sponsoring might be—just might be, you understand—a Communist and, well, do I have to tell you what would happen?"

"All right, Jim, I can't argue with you. It's one of those things I don't like to think about."

"Yes, I suppose it is," he said with a short laugh.

"But still," I said, "it's pretty hard to believe a gal like Ginny would actually go through with a thing like that."

"Don't be horrified, laddie. Happens all the time—best-regulated families and all that nonsense. You see, Bob, another thing—Ginny liked money. The more the better. It was all very noble of her to say she only wanted that much money from me to teach me a lesson. But I knew better. The more money Ginny could get her hands on the more she liked it. She was damn near pathological about it and she wasn't fooling me one bit about teaching me lessons or anything else."

"All right," I said. "I'll take your word for it. But I still don't see why you're telling me all this. What's the point?"

"Oh," he said lightly, "nothing so odd about that. After all, why shouldn't a fellow confide in his best friend?"

"Look here, Jim," I said. "Let's cut out the goddamn double-talk. I don't particularly like all this hinting around. What do you say we skip it once and for all? If there's anything I can help with, O.K.—name it and I'll try to do what I can. Otherwise, I'd just as soon—"

"What's the matter, aren't you even interested in hearing

the rest of the script?" he grinned. "I thought you'd be sort of interested."

"You know something?" I said. "I really did have the idea you were trying to pull some gag when you started all this. But now I'm actually beginning to believe you, do you realize that?"

"Yes, of course," he said calmly. "Why not? It's the truth. Why shouldn't you believe me?"

"No, you don't understand," I said. "I mean about the other too—"

"You mean about . . . ah . . . pushing Ginny over the cliff?" he smiled. "Of course. I understand. As I say, why shouldn't you believe me? It's perfectly true."

"I swear to God," I told him seriously, "if I hadn't had so much personal experience with the way that mind of yours works I wouldn't know what the hell to think about anything by this time."

"Well," he laughed. "You'll soon know, laddie. As soon as I've finished."

"Fine, I can hardly wait," I said. "But you don't mind a small comment, do you? It really is a messy picture. In fact, if you'll allow me to be truthful about it, I wish I could go all the way back to where I was before you started showing it to me. It may sound funny to you, but the fact is I used to think Ginny was a damn nice gal."

"Sure, I know," he nodded. "Lots of guys around town apparently did."

I started to say something but decided to let that one pass.

"Anyway," he said after another moment. "Got it all straight so far?"

I assured him I had it straight and he went on.

As I told you, Bob, Ginny was a very sharp little operator—pound for pound one of the sharpest I've ever run into in my life. But I've become a fairly sharp operator myself over the last fifteen or twenty years. So—when she told me all about her little plan for my future life as her ex-husband—it began to sink in that it would be damned good tactics for me to start walking very slowly and watching my step very, very carefully if I wanted to get out from under. At which point, sore as I was, I managed to control myself enough to tell her I'd like to have a few days to think the whole thing over. She was very gracious about it, told me she realized how a man might need a little time to think when he was in a corner like that.

Well, as soon as I began to examine my position, I saw I was really over a barrel. Of course I could have got off the spot immediately—all I needed was a hundred thousand dollars to hand over to her. However, since I neither had it, nor would have been willing to hand it over to her if I had, that was out. By now I didn't care who got the divorce, just so I could be rid of her. But the longer I thought about it the more I saw I was going to have one hell of a time untangling myself. Finally I decided to have another talk with her and see if I couldn't get her to change her mind—about the money, that is. I told her she could go ahead and get her divorce, that I was even willing to let her get it on the grounds that I had been the one who'd committed adultery if that was what she wanted. The only thing I asked was to be let out in one piece and be allowed to go on making my living.

Well, I got exactly nowhere. All she did was laugh at me.

"Poor Jim," she said. "You don't really care about a measly hundred thousand dollars, do you? A man as ingenious as you! Why, you shouldn't have any trouble making that much in practically no time at all. You can even pay it off in small installments if you like. Say, five or ten thousand a year? Doesn't that sound fair?" And she kept on that way, kind of gloating and rubbing it in, until I lost control and next thing I knew I had my hands on her throat and was snarling that

I'd strangle her to death right that minute if she tried to go through with extorting any money from me.

Of course, as soon as I came to my senses and realized what I was doing, I let go of her. But the funny part of it is, it turned out to be the thing that ultimately gave me the key to the entire situation. You see, Bob, there were these two completely divergent sides to Ginny. She was an extremely complex girl. In many ways she was about as peculiar a combination of traits as I've ever heard of anywhere. Everyone who knew her was aware of how coldly brilliant and clever she was; when it came to business she could be downright ruthless—could be, hell. She was.

But there was another side to her, which almost nobody ever saw because mostly she pushed it down inside herself and kept it well hidden. It was almost as if she had never really grown up in this one respect because underneath that sophisticated woman-of-the-world facade she had cultivated, she was still a little girl in some ways. A very shrewd little girl who'd been clever enough to figure out that most people aren't very well organized and that as long as they went on following certain rules of the game—which most of us actually do—she could outplay 'em right and left. Because her brain functioned like a computer. And yet, with it all, since she had never quite managed to grow up, there was a certain naïveté in her which at times caused her to react quite unpredictably to the most ordinary signs of elementary human behavior. And the result was that people sometimes scared the hell out of her. This is kind of hard to explain. What it amounts to, I suppose, is that she was a little like one of those child chess prodigies. Actually that's pretty close to it, because you see, Ginny had life figured out almost as if it were a chess game—and the one thing that baffled her was irrationality. At the first sign of things not working out according to pure logic she was liable to get scared out of her wits. Which was exactly what happened when I threatened to kill her. Because knowing this childlike quality of hers, I'd always been pretty gentle with her after I discovered how frightened she was of any sort of physical violence. Now here she was, having figured out everything she was going to force me to do—just as if it were a real game of chess we'd been playing—and all at once I'd made a move that had nothing to do with the rules, you under-stand—which was too much for her. It stopped her dead and, though I hadn't planned it at all, it was the one thing, of all the things I might have done, that gave me the out I was looking for.

He stopped and looked at me.

"What are you shaking your head like that for?" he asked.

"I find it pretty hard to believe that Ginny wouldn't have known you didn't really mean what you were saying," I said. "After all, she couldn't have been childish enough not to realize you'd only threatened to kill her because you were sore as hell—not that you didn't have good reason to be sore, but still. . . ."

"You know?" he said. "I'll be damned if you don't remind me of Ginny yourself in some ways. You've got that same odd combination of cleverness and perception—but there are times when you can be awfully childish."

"Thanks a lot for the free character analysis, but if you don't mind, I fail to see the connection."

He gave me a sarcastic smile and inclined his head. "You've simply overlooked one trifling detail. Certainly she realized I was sore. I was. Sore as hell. But what doesn't seem to cross your mind is the obvious fact—which she un-derstood immediately—that I meant it. If she hadn't agreed to let up I'd have killed her then and there."

There was nothing to say to this; only now, for the first time since he had started telling me all this, I realized he was in deadly earnest. He was watching my face and sud-denly he nodded briefly.

"You see, laddie," he went on, "that was the one thing Ginny hadn't counted on and, as I say, it was the only thing I could have done to make her stop and think it over. Which leads neatly to the next plot point. This has to do with another serious blind spot in Ginny's makeup." He broke off abruptly, cocked his head to one side as if he were listening to something, and suddenly grinned at me. "If you'll excuse the involuntary pun, old boy?"

"Pun?" I repeated blankly.

"Makeup," he said. "Virginia Warren, Inc. Remember? But I assure you, laddie, I didn't intend it that way—it just sort of popped out." He was still grinning and I couldn't help a swift feeling of revulsion at his pointing out the idiotic connection in such an oafish way. For no reason at all I suddenly remembered one of the newspaper accounts of the "condition" of Ginny's body when it was recovered . . .

"Very funny," I said.

"Sorry," he said. He stopped grinning but I got the impression of a man trying to appear contrite when he did not really feel that way at all.

"In any case," he was saying, "about this blind spot of Ginny's—are you listening, Bob?"

I looked over and saw him staring at me out of those flat, opaque eyes of his and I found myself wondering why I had never noticed how hard they could be. All at once I recalled an incident that took place in New Caledonia some months after I got to know Jim a little better.

. . . Actually, even the word incident is an overstatement. Nothing much happened. One morning Jim was summoned for an interview with our commanding officer, a lieutenant general known for his irascible disposition. In itself, of course, there was nothing noteworthy about that, since at that stage of the Pacific war people around Noumea were all a little jumpy and on edge. The state of affairs in the combined services down there during that period is best summed up by four initials which were used to describe the unutterably fouled-up way things were going. MCSO was what a man would say whenever anything went cockeyed—as everything seemed to be going most of the time. It was one more variation on the snafu theme and all it meant was Mass Confusion Slightly Organized; which is not very funny now, though at the time it had seemed a humorous enough comment on what we lived with day after gummed-up day.

At any rate, when an orderly showed up with a message for Colonel Peterson to report immediately to General Ingram who was waiting for him over at ComSerOnSoPac, everybody in the outfit knew what it was about. Someone had fouled up a decoding job the day before and, while the results were not exactly disastrous, they were not particularly pleasant. Jim left immediately for General Ingram's headquarters and as his footsteps crunched down the gravel path leading from the front door of our communications shack Sergeant Lippman grinned wryly over at me and said, "Looks like the Colonel's gonna get his ass ate out for sure, huh, Captain?"

An hour or so afterwards Jim returned and walked to his desk without a word to anyone. A moment later he buzzed for me and when I walked into his cubicle of an office I found him sitting behind his desk wearing the expression of a man who has just come through an ordeal. I thought nothing of it at first when he announced curtly that from now on things had better tighten up and that he would hold me personally responsible for seeing that they did. After all, though we had become rather friendly by then, I knew better than to think that had anything to do with my duties while I was under his command. In the service these little unpleasantnesses were more or less taken for granted. A harassed superior officer could always relieve his tensions by lashing out at the nearest scapegoat at hand, who would then get rid of his resentment by turning on someone a little further down the chain of command. Ordinarily there was a sort of wry humor about the whole thing and no one took it very seriously.

"Very well, sir," I answered when he finished what I thought of as blowing off steam. I waited to see if there was anything else and then when he turned to some papers on his desk I made a small joke of some sort about his interview with General Ingram. It wasn't really anything, just one of those meaningless pleasantries a fellow might make under those circumstances. I was astonished when he looked back up at me and I saw the look in his eyes.

"That'll do now, Captain," he snapped. "Get out!" That was all but it was enough to get me out of there in a hurry. For the rest of the day I had an uneasy feeling whenever I thought about the way his eyes had looked when he dismissed me. They were as cold and flat and opaque as the eyes of a wolf looking out at you from between the bars of a cage; and though he apologized to me that evening, so that I put it out of mind and ultimately forgot it, it suddenly occurred to me now, as he stared coldly over at me, that I had been looking at the eyes of a man who—given the proper circumstances—would probably not hesitate to murder someone if he thought it necessary . . .

As I thought of it now, though, it seemed faraway and—well, cliché. The whole incident had a sort of melodramatic quality and I tried to shrug it off. But I could not quite manage it.

"Yes, Jim," I said, "I'm listening. You were talking about blind spots . . . Go on."

Well actually, he resumed, I touched on it once a long time ago when I mentioned—or did I—that Ginny was extraordinarily preoccupied with her looks. As you know, Bob, Ginny was a very handsome woman. I think I remember telling you once that she was not quite beautiful but not far from it—something like that. Point is, it was that 'not-*quite*-

beautiful that caused her to behave the way she did—in all sorts of unexpected little ways. Big ways too, far as that goes—because I believe it also had a lot to do with her whole sexual drive. You know, she seemed to be trying to prove something to herself, and naturally a perfectly valid way of proving to yourself how—ah . . . irresistible you are is through admiration—or, to call a certain type of admiration by a one-syllable word, sex.

Anyway, what I'm getting at is that because she must have realized she wasn't really beautiful—after all, beauty was her profession; she sold it, you see, as a commodity—because she knew that, Ginny used to put in a great deal of her time and energy trying to convince herself that she *was* beautiful. It seemed to mean an awful lot to her. But she never could quite make the grade—at least not to her own satisfaction, though she'd spend hours fixing herself up and primping before a mirror and never would dream of being seen in public unless she was all done up and dressed to the hilt.

I used to kid her about it now and then, shortly after we were first married. But I quit when I began to see this was no laughing matter to her. Nevertheless all this intense preoccupation with her looks gave me an important clue. You see, I knew by now that the one thing on earth Ginny needed, the thing she desperately had to have—I believe it was probably the single most important thing on earth for her—was to be told she was beautiful . . .

So—there it was. Now that I'd . . . ah . . . demonstrated for her that it wouldn't be such a smart idea to go through with her little blackmail plan, I had two choices. On the one hand I could let her divorce me. But on the other hand I sort of liked the position I was in—after all, Ginny was a wealthy girl and I suppose by that time I had kind of got used to money. Not that I couldn't have made a pretty fair amount on my own, but still. Anyway, I finally decided to play along for a while and see what might turn up.

But—in order to do the thing right I had to convince her

that things between us would be the way they had been when we first got married. More or less, that is. And the only way that could be accomplished, of course, would be for me to sell myself to her again—almost as if we'd just met each other for the first time, you understand. In other words, I would have to put aside any thought of personal pride, or dignity, or any of that sort of nonsense, and unemotionally devote myself to the job of making her fall in love with me again. Treat it as a job, you see, simply go at it that way and handle it as skillfully as I'd try to handle any other job. After all, I'd already done it once—why shouldn't I be able to again? Besides I really had a good-sized stake in doing it well this time, you understand.

So—I decided to stop indulging myself in what might turn out to be expensive histrionics, and utilize everything I knew about her to map out a campaign designed to win her back as my everlovin' wife again.

Which is precisely what I did, laddie.

All this was, as I've said, entirely unemotional and as a result quite effective—if I do say so myself. I did everything I knew she would have wanted me to and, since I already knew pretty well everything she wanted, I could for the most part do it before she even asked me to. And after I'd managed to get her over the effects of that one big fight it wasn't as hard a job as it might sound. The whole campaign took a couple of years but in the end I succeeded perfectly. Along the way, of course, there were times when I'd—ah—flag a bit. That is to say, physically, you understand. But at those times she'd contrive to get out and have a bit of sport on the side now and then. Also, I never again let on that I had any idea of what she was up to on those occasions, and while she probably knew I suspected what she was up to she no doubt assumed I'd become reconciled to the idea. After all, there's nothing so spectacularly novel about it as a piece of folk-ways, when you examine the situation with a certain tolerance.

In any case, by the time a couple of years had gone by,

with me behaving as the perfect gent at all times, we'd arrived at a point where she trusted me implicitly—scarcely made a move without me. Why, toward the end she even started cutting down on her extra-curricular sexual activities, believe it or not—after all, there I was, ready and available and doing my best to please, and no matter how you slice it a thing like that is always more convenient when you've got it waiting for you at home, as they say.

Not that this spot of . . . ah . . . reform on her part wasn't something of a mixed blessing in many ways—because after a while I began feeling like the old guy in the gag. Remember the one? About the old boy who decides to kill his young wife off by giving her an overdose of sex and then winds up in a wheel chair watching her go around radiant and blooming while he sits there cackling to himself: "That's O.K., honey—you go right on smiling but in another week or so you'll be dead."

Jim was chuckling but I could not even look him in the eye now. There was something so nasty in his use of the tired old chestnut in this account of his quiet, devious plot to murder Ginny that I felt a real revulsion. I think I managed to hide my feelings but I have no way of knowing for certain.

He resumed a moment later and this time I listened quietly until he came to what seemed to be the end.

Once he had won Ginny back as his wife—as he put it—Jim remained the model husband right up until the moment of her death. Completely and assiduously devoted to her in every detail, he hovered over her, lavished her with attention and flattery, helped her with all sorts of irksome problems connected with her business—in short, he became a combination of father, lover, nurse, husband, business-counselor, and anything else she seemed to want. This went on for

nearly another year. Then one pleasant spring day they decided to take a short vacation. They had these friends who
owned a model dairy farm upstate and their plan was that
after a three or four day drive up through the Catskills,
stopping off wherever they might find a place along the
road—it was before the season and they would be practically alone the whole time—they would end up at their
friends' place for the weekend. The fact was, Jim told me,
that this little jaunt was his idea but he was extremely careful to plant the seed of it in such a way as to make Ginny
believe she had thought of it herself. Then, a day or two
after leaving New York, he began telling her about the old
Catskill House. The place was now a dilapidated ruin being
torn down as part of a State Park project; but in the early
part of the century the Catskill House had been regarded as
one of the wonders of the world. When Jim told Ginny about
the astounding view to be had from the nearly mile-high cliff
on which the hotel was situated, she asked him if they could
have a look at it. Jim pretended to try to dissuade her. It
was, he pointed out, quite a few miles out of their way.
Besides, there were only several more hours of daylight left,
which meant they might have to drive quite late until they
could find a place to stay overnight. Also, he told her, he had
heard that the building itself was probably nothing more
than a ruin by now. And so on. But the more he demurred
the more Ginny insisted on going—as of course he knew she
would. They got up there about an hour before sundown. It
was a weekday in early April, and the tourist season would
not begin for at least another couple of months. The place
was deserted. Then—well, then he contrived to maneuver
Ginny near the edge of the cliff on the pretext of wanting to
point out the location of their friends' farm. And as she
peered out over the edge he stepped quietly behind her and
gave her a quick shove.

That was all there was to it.

Of course, in compressing his story this way, I have

omitted a number of details. Such as, for example, Jim's description of the sound Ginny made when she realized what was happening to her and especially as she felt herself dropping over the edge of the nearly sheer cliff.

"It started out as a sort of shrill scream," he told me, almost as if he were describing some sound-effect he might have wanted for the television show, "but then as she started falling it turned into a cross between a deep sigh and a kind of a moan—almost a wail. Funny—I remember the line about woman wailing for her demon lover kind of popping into my mind for a split second, along with all sorts of other confused thoughts. And all the time you could hear that moan, or wail, dying away down there and it was the saddest sound you've ever heard in your life—not at all frightened-sounding as you might have expected, but just plain sad, sad, sad. For one instant—much as I hated her guts—I think I'd have done anything in the world to bring her back. I got down on my hands and knees and looked down the side of the cliff and it must have been almost immediately after I'd pushed her over because I saw her hit a rock partway down there and bounce off and then hit something again and her body went on falling end over end and hitting again till a long time later—or anyway it seemed like a hell of a long time —she finally went out of sight way down below and that was it. A few little stones and pebbles and bits of earth and stuff went rattling down the side of the cliff but pretty soon even that stopped and then it was suddenly very quiet. There wasn't a sound anywhere and I looked up and saw the glow from where the sun was setting behind me. There was some kind of large bird flying around up against the sky—hawk, I guess . . . I crawled back and got to my feet and then discovered I was trembling all over and my knees were so shaky I could barely make it back to where I'd parked the car about twenty or thirty yards away . . ."

There was a good deal more of this sort of thing, but

finally Jim stopped talking and sat there looking at me as if he were waiting for something. All I could do was stare at him in a kind of dumb horror.

Suddenly he asked me a question.

"What?" I asked. "What did you say?" My whole body felt oddly numb.

"I said have you got any . . . ah . . . comments you feel like making?"

"Comments?" I asked, staring stupidly at him. "What the hell kind of comments, for God's sake?"

He was eyeing me intently, as if he were being very careful not to miss the slightest flicker of my expression; I got a feeling of cat-like watchfulness in the way he stared at me.

"I'm sort of curious about your reactions to the script," he said smiling but with his eyes glued on mine. "You know. Whether you think it holds together," his lips curling in a smile but his eyes narrowly watchful. "Sure you haven't got anything you want to tell me, Bob?"

"Look," I answered, getting up out of my chair. "I haven't got the slightest idea of what the hell you're driving at." I heard my voice rising but I could not control it. My body was trembling uncontrollably as I went on. "I don't know yet what you expect me to believe or think about all this. Sure, sure, I know—people commit murder all over the place, we put on a show about it every week. I heard you, about the best-regulated families and all that crap. But Christ—Ginny and you! Why the hell are you telling me all this crazy stuff? Why me, for God's sake?"

"I told you before," he answered, his voice quite calm and low. "You're my best friend. Why shouldn't I tell my best friend? It really did happen just the way I've told you. Take my word for it, Bob—everything I've told you tonight is true, believe me."

"All right, I believe you then." My voice sounded strange to my own ears. There was something about the way he kept staring at me out of those flat, hard wolf's eyes of his that was beginning to work on me and drive me into a sort of panic.

"All right!" I shouted at him. "I tell you I believe you! What the hell more do you want?"

His eyes remained as opaque as ever but now the corners of his mouth twitched slightly, as if he were enjoying himself.

"You really don't know what I'm waiting for you to tell me?" he asked softly, his eyes still boring into mine. "Don't you see the one thing the script needs?"

"How the hell can I know anything if all you do is sit there staring at me like that?" I shouted.

"Bob," he said very quietly. "Sit down and let me ask you a question."

"Anything," I said. "Go on and ask it," sitting down in my chair again. "Go ahead, give me some idea what the hell this is all about."

He hesitated for a brief moment, as if he were trying to select his words.

"Just one thing," he said at last, looking back into my eyes, peering into them as if he were trying to watch my mind operate. His earlier bantering manner was completely gone now. "Just this. . . . When was the first time you ever fucked Ginny?"

"The first time I ev—when was the . . . *me?*"

His expression did not change and I stared at him with my jaw hanging.

"Yes, Bob. . . . You," he said evenly.

It seemed to take a long time before I could answer him. I walked over to where he sat.

"Listen, Jim," I said very intensely. "You're crazy. Do you hear what I'm telling you? You're stark, raving, twisted crazy. You're right smack out of your mind, do you understand? Ginny and I never even so much as thought of touching each oth—"

"Don't lie to me, Bob," he cut in quietly. He looked up at me and his eyes narrowed slightly.

"I'm not lying," and now my own voice became quiet. "Listen to me," I said. "I can only tell you this, there's no way I can get you to accept it unless you'll take my word I'm not lying to you. There's no point in my lying—what'd be the use of it now? Believe me, Jim, you're absolutely dead wrong about this. You're as wrong as you've ever been in your life. I never so much as thought of laying a hand on Ginny. I never had one thing to do with her that you didn't know about at the time. That's all there is to it, and it's the whole truth, so help me."

His expression barely flickered; but the hard, cold, empty, watchful stare was still in his eyes.

"You know?" he said flatly. "I'd damn near believe you at that—except for one thing."

"What one thing?"

"Ginny." He looked at me. "Ginny told me herself. She told me quite a while ago. In fact, that was what that big fight of ours was about. I told you, I'd known she was cheating before then. But when she told me about you. . . . Well, anyway—that was why I almost killed her right then and there, see? But I decided I'd wait. I've had my eyes on you for a long time, laddie—almost two and a half years before I finally decided she'd either tipped you off about having told me or else given you a fast brush, as she had with so many other fellows like yourself . . ." and he went on with a long, complicated tale about having hired private detectives to watch me, elaborate traps he had carefully baited for me— pouring out all the sick, poisonous suspicions he had been harboring over the past two years or more.

I stood there appalled, trying to assimilate all the things he was saying.

". . . so that was why I finally had to kill her," he concluded. "At first I was going to kill you too. Oh sure—I thought of it, had it all worked out. But after I got to thinking it over I decided I'd take care of Ginny first. I could always get around to you sooner or later, as long as I had you right under my eye where I could get at you whenever I got ready. And meantime there was still this one thing I had to know anyway—and you were the one person who could tell me. So I thought I might as well wait till I—"

By this time I had found my voice again.

"Look, Jim, listen to me!" I said again. "I don't understand any of this and I'm not going to pretend I do. The only thing I can even vaguely put together out of everything you've told me tonight is that for some reason of her own Ginny wanted to hurt you—badly, I mean. She was a smart girl, as you say, and she must have decided that I was one guy you liked well enough to be really hurt by. Something like that— I don't know what the hell it's all about—but it *has* to be something like that, can't you see? My God! You've got to believe me! It's the truth, can't you see I'm not lying about this?"

I felt that some of this was finally beginning to sink in. I went on before he could interrupt.

"Look, I know there's no way I can ever prove this to you—now that she's dead. But let me ask you a question. What would you rather believe—which would make you feel better? Why go on believing something that bothers you that much? What do you gain by it? Because so help me, Jim, it's a lie—neither of us will ever know now why the lie was told, no matter what we might guess about it—but it is a lie! Believe me, this is the truth—why not accept it and have some peace?"

He looked away and shook his head like a man coming up out of water. I heard him take a deep breath and a moment later he let out a heavy sigh. Then he turned back to me but there was no way to tell from his expression whether I had convinced him or not.

"You want to know why I didn't kill you, Bob?" he asked

after a few more moments. "You want me to tell you what I wanted to find out—the thing that you were the one guy I could ask about?"

"What, Jim?" I asked.

He looked up into my eyes again but I still could not tell whether he had believed me.

"What is it?" I repeated. "What did you want to find out?"

"I'll tell you," he said slowly. "Don't worry, I'll tell you. . . . Look—let's forget all about this other. It doesn't really matter to me anymore whether you did or didn't make it with Ginny. Hell with it—I don't care anymore. But I want you to level with me now—because this is the one thing I *do* have to know. Have you got this straight, Bob? I don't care if you slept with her or not—I mean that. So you can tell me the truth about this. I . . . have to . . . find out! Will you level with me?"

"Anything you want to know, that I can tell you about—I'll tell you."

I sat down in my chair and waited.

"O.K.," he said. "All I want to know is—were you able to satisfy her? Now wait a second—I want the truth, Bob! It's the thing I've got to know so take your time and don't lie to me because if you do, I swear to God I'll kill you right now!"

"How much time do you want me to take before I answer you?" I looked at him and, oddly enough, I was not even frightened now, though I was perfectly aware that he meant what he had just said.

"All the time you need," he said flatly. "Just so it's the truth when you do answer."

"All right," I said calmly. "I'm ready right now."

He nodded.

"The only answer I can give you is this," I said. "I can't answer you because I never had anything to do with Ginny that would give me the information you want. You can kill me if you want, but that's all I know to tell you."

For the first time now his expression changed. His eyes began to look like human eyes as he looked across at me. Troubled, pained, deeply hurt and—somehow—and now I began to understand some of why—bewildered; but the wolf-look was gone.

"All right, Bob," he said quietly and I finally knew he believed me. He shook his head rapidly as though he were trying to wipe something out of his mind. "That's enough—I'll take your word for it. . . . But Jesus Christ!" shaking his head again and frowning at the floor. "Why the hell should she have lied to me about a thing like that? What the hell was there in it for her?"

I watched him for a moment before answering.

"It doesn't make much sense," I said. "As I told you, we'll probably never understand it altogether. The only thing I can even guess at is what I've already told you—that she knew this was one way to hit at you really hard and—well, she used it."

"She sure as hell used it all right," he said, staring down at a spot between his feet. "Why, she even told me you were the only man who'd ever really satisfied her—that you were the one man who—"

"All right, Jim," I interrupted. "Never mind going into all that—I've got the picture pretty clear . . ."

Just then a thought flashed across my mind. You see, I knew Jim Peterson. I knew how his mind worked. I had seen the way it clicked whenever we had worked together on a script and I knew there was nothing he was not capable of trying, no matter how grotesque or far-fetched, if he felt it would add to the interest of his program. Actually it was one of the principal reasons for the original success of *Suspicion;* but now I suddenly wondered . . .

"Jim," I said.

He looked up at me.

"You didn't make all this up, did you?"

"Make it up?" he asked. "Make what up?"

"All this about Ginny telling you about our having—you know, about our having had an affair?"

"Hell no," he said. "*That's* the truth. Why would I make up a story like that? Why should I take the trouble to—?"

"I don't know, Jim," I answered. "I really don't know. But what do you mean—*that's* the truth? What about the rest of it?"

"The rest of it?"

"You know what I mean," I said impatiently.

All at once I thought of Ginny and I was almost overcome by a sudden feeling of repugnance as I thought about whatever it was that prompted her to tell him what she had told him . . .

"Holy Christ!" I was not aware of having spoken aloud until I saw him looking curiously at me.

"What's the trouble, Bob?" he asked.

"God Almighty!" I said. "What an evil creature she really must have been! I'm beginning to understand now why you did what you did. I won't say I know exactly how you felt—and I can't say I agree with it. But I think I'm beginning to understand why you had to do it . . . Only thing I wish is that you'd never told me about it because now I—"

"Never told you about what, Bob?" he said. His face was expressionless as he looked at me with arched eyebrows.

"Why, about Ginny—about what you—you know, what you did to her. The whole thing. About up there on that cliff."

He was staring at me now as if I had suddenly started barking like a dog.

"What's the matter with you?" he asked in a tone of mild alarm. "What are you talking about?" He was looking at me in innocent wonder.

All at once I began to feel as if I were going out of my mind. "About killing her!" I said, my voice beginning to rise again. "What you've been telling me—about having pushed her over the edge of that cliff! Jim! What the hell's going on here? You just got through telling me the whole damn thing and now you look at me as if I'd made it up myself. What are you trying to—"

"Hey, hey, boy—take it e-a-s-y," he said. "What are you trying to say, Bob? I never said anything about pushing Ginny over any cliff. It was an accident, you know that. Get hold of yourself, laddie—good Lord, you don't want to make a fool of yourself, do you? It was an accident, Bob. Everybody knows it was an accident. Get a grip on yourself, boy! Want people to think you're going off your rocker? Good Lord! I guess you do need a little vacation—look at you! That damn show has really got you down, hasn't it?"

It was such a convincing performance that if I had not actually been there and heard what had gone before I might have been taken in. By now I could not tell what was true—not about the murder he had so graphically described to me, nor whether I had really convinced him about the innocence of my relationship with Ginny—nor even whether she had actually ever told him the lie he had just told me about. And now as he went on asking me solicitously what was wrong with me and why I was behaving so jumpily—those were his exact words—I suddenly felt I had had enough.

"Shut up, God damn you!" I practically screamed.

He looked at me and raised his eyebrows.

"Shut up!" I shouted again. "I don't want to hear another goddamn word about it, you hear me?"

"Why, all right, Bob," he said, as if to humor me.

After a moment I regained control of myself.

"Listen," I said. "I don't care about anything anymore. I'll never open my mouth about any of this—not to anybody, understand? But for God's sake, why the hell did you tell me all this?"

He suddenly laughed. I stood there staring at him until he stopped laughing.

"I just thought it might . . . ah . . . stimulate you," he said, still smiling. "I think you'll have to admit it's not a bad script, especially when you consider it just came off the cuff that way."

"I see," I said. "Well, as long as we're talking about it as a script, though—there is one thing missing, you know. After all, *Suspicion* has a format and we like to keep the show uniform in that one respect at least."

"What respect?" he smiled. "What's missing?"

"Humor," I told him. "There's no humor in your script."

"Why, Bob!" he said. "Mean to tell me you don't get it?" His face took on a look of mock concern. "I guess you really did miss it . . ." Pursing his lips and looking off into space. "Let's see now. Let me see if there isn't some way we could underline it without pointing it up too much . . ."

"Come on—what's so goddamn funny?" I said. "What's the big joke?"

"Just that, don't you see?" He looked blandly at me. "The audience will never know at the end of the show whether it actually happened or didn't. The entire . . . ah . . . credibility of the script hangs on that one small point—now do you see the humor of it? I admit it's a little subtle but. . . ."

"Yes, Jim." I gave him one last long look. "Yes—I guess I do see it. Very, very clever. It ought to make a great show—only I may as well tell you right now, you're going to have to get yourself another boy. As of tonight I'm finished. Forget the vacation. *Suspicion* is now in the market for a new producer."

And before he could say anything else I opened the door, walked out, and slammed it behind me. The last thing I remember is the way he raised his eyebrows as I left.

I have never seen Jim since that night. Of course I hear things about him here and there around town. Not long ago I heard he had sold Virginia Warren, Inc. I don't remember the exact figure but I know it was a very high one; so I suppose Jim will not have to be worrying about money for quite some time to come. Meantime he has gone back to producing *Suspicion* and the rating is, I'm told, higher than ever—which is only natural since he is unquestionably one of the most capable men in his field. As far as that goes, I suppose Jim Peterson would be successful at almost anything he turned his hand to—he is that kind of person. Still, I don't envy him. It might sound silly for me to say that. It may even sound foolish when I say I have never regretted walking out on *Suspicion* the way I did—especially in view of the fact that I will probably never get a show as good as that again.

All I can say is, I'm not the least bit sorry. What I want to do is forget I've ever heard the name Jim Peterson or had anything to do with anything he's ever had anything to do with—including *Suspicion*. Sure, it's a first-rate television show. But I don't want any part of it. Too tough on the nerves. I'd like to hang onto my sanity for a little while longer; hard as that may be nowadays . . .